THE LON[...]

by

Margaret Brazear

Copyright © Margaret Brazear 2023

The past is filled with shadows
But the longest shadow follows you forever

CHAPTER ONE

Just one more week until Ava would be Mrs Ryan Kenyon. One more week before she could wear that beautiful dress, or would it better be described as a gown? It certainly looked like Ava's idea of a medieval gown, with its layers of fine net and lace, its white silk embroidery entwined with pearls. It even had laces to fasten it at the back, so that she needed someone to lace it up for her, just like those ladies in the Tudor court.

It was presently hidden away in the wardrobe of her future mother-in-law, Liz Kenyon. Liz and her husband, Joe, Ryan's father, had been so good to Ava. She was brought up by her Gran and since she died, some three years ago, Ava hadn't had any relatives of her own at all. Liz and Joe had been like the parents she never had and she thought the world of them.

Ava had been there today, trying on the entire outfit, dress, veil, headdress, the whole thing, just to be sure. The only thing missing was the bouquet; she couldn't pick that up until the last minute. Gold roses was what she had chosen and they hadn't been easy to get, not cheap either. Still, it would only happen once; Ava was sure of that. She loved Ryan too much to ever let him go and he loved her too; she knew that, was certain of it.

She'd only recently found the shoes, in a little shop in the old part of town, after searching for weeks for just the right ones. Most brides seemed to have silver or synthetic glass, Cinderella type of thing, but Ava didn't want that. She wanted white, but not leather; she wanted satin and they just weren't in fashion. She had scoured the internet, as well as every shoe shop she could think of. But she wanted new, not second hand, and she was almost prepared to give up and choose something else, when she found them.

It was a funny little shop, full of knick-knacks, ornaments, pots and pans, mostly used items. But, although these shoes were in the window among all the used stuff, they were new, still in their box and as though fate had taken a hand, they were just Ava's size. The assistant had started to tell her the story behind them, but Ava had silenced her with a raised hand and a 'hush'. She didn't want to know what tragedy or heartache might have caused the bride who had originally purchased them, to never take them out of their box.

"It's all right, dear," said the elderly lady who owned the shop, suddenly appearing from a dark corner. "They belonged to my daughter.

She bought them then found a pair she liked better, so these never got worn."

"Oh," said Ava. "And is she...?"

"Still married? Yes, dear and she has children and grandchildren. Heading for her fiftieth wedding anniversary soon."

That pleased Ava, made her even more determined to wear these shoes. They were obviously blessed, fated to find their way onto Ava's feet.

Today she'd been able to see them with the rest of the bridal outfit, or perhaps it was just an excuse to try it all on again.

"You look beautiful, Ava," said Liz. "Just amazing."

She smiled but Ava could see the sadness behind that smile; there was always sadness behind that smile. She wondered if Liz's personal tragedy would ever let her go, but she wasn't going to let that spoil her big day. Nothing was going to spoil her big day.

Excitement fluttered through her stomach; she had never been so excited in all her life. In truth, excitement wasn't an emotion she found easy to summon; if one didn't get excited, then the chances of disappointment were greatly reduced. She only wished her grandmother were here to see it. She also wished Ryan's little sister were here to be bridesmaid, as once again this afternoon, his mother had wept for her lost daughter, missing for twelve years, since the age of seven.

Knowing she was more than likely dead, Liz always hoped to find her body, to be able to bury her. Ava didn't really understand that; they must know she was dead and she had to be buried somewhere. She always believed the family were better off remaining in ignorance of Melanie's cause of death. Why did they want to know the horror she must have suffered? But not understanding didn't keep Ava from sympathising and she wasn't yet a mother. She might feel differently when she was.

Ava was a follower of spiritualism and she firmly believed that a dead body was nothing more than an empty shell, that the essence of who someone was in life lived on, in spirit, without any of the pain they might have suffered in this life.

She had once tried to convince Liz of that, but she couldn't quite understand her point of view. Ava wouldn't push it; she respected that faith was a personal thing and something one had to sort out for oneself.

Today it was the usual, the bridesmaids' dresses that had set Liz off. Ava had stashed them all in Liz's spare wardrobe, together with her wedding dress.

"My Melanie should be bridesmaid," she said.

Ava knew what was coming, she'd heard it all before and although her heart went out to Liz, this was her day and she wanted to be the centre of attention, but she shook herself out of her selfish thoughts.

Ryan's father was to give her away, as she had no male relative of her own to play the role, and she only had three adult bridesmaids. She didn't want any little ones, as that would only serve as a reminder to Ryan's parents of the little girl who was missing from the festivities.

There were photos of Melanie all over the house. She had pretty blonde curls, blue eyes and a mischievous smile. Ava didn't know a lot about children, but Melanie looked to be a nice child, a child one could easily love.

One picture clearly showed Melanie's crossed over bottom teeth and Liz had, as always, caught Ava looking at it.

"She was booked to have a brace fitted to straighten those teeth," she said. "I forgot to cancel and they sent me a bill. Would you believe that? I wonder if she ever got them done."

Ava made no reply. She had heard this before from Ryan's mother and she never had an answer for her. Sometimes she would accept that her daughter was dead and she just wanted to bury her remains, other times, like this one, she seemed to think she was still alive somewhere. It was heart wrenching.

Ava regularly attended the medium evenings at the Spiritualist Church in Cambridge, always hoping Melanie might come through and she could pass that comfort along to Liz, but it never happened. That meant nothing, of course, as there were always lots of people there, all hoping one of their relatives would be the one and time was limited.

Ava thought the one thing that would make her celebration complete would be if Melanie could be found. That would make everything perfect, even if she wasn't found alive, just to give peace of mind to Ryan's parents.

Thinking about it brought a tear to Ava's eye and as she turned into the drive of the house she had shared with Ryan for the past two years, she thought it would be a nice idea, after the wedding, to have Melanie photoshopped into one of the photographs. She'd see what he thought about it.

His car was already here, so it must be later than she thought. She wondered if he'd been in long enough to start dinner as she was hungry now. Liz had given her lunch, but her idea of lunch wasn't Ava's. She was one of those people who never seemed to put on weight, no matter how much she ate, and she had got used to eating hearty meals. Liz, on the other hand, thought a salad with an egg was enough to fill anyone up.

Ava unlocked the front door, stepped into the brightly lit hallway, and noticed straight away that the television was silent. There was a light coming from the lounge and it was unusual for it to be this quiet; Ryan always put the television on the minute he got in.

"I'm home," she said, as she appeared at the living room doorway. "You ok?"

He turned his head to stare at her from his position on the sofa, where he leaned back with his arms folded. Where was the smile with which he always greeted her? He would always get to his feet, give her a hug and a kiss; she looked forward to it.

"What's wrong?" she asked.

She hurried to sit beside him, gave him a kiss on the cheek, but she got no response. He looked angry, if anything, and that simply wasn't like Ryan.

The first thought that flitted through her mind was that he had changed his mind about marrying her, but then she pushed the idea away. Only last night in bed, after making love, he had told her how much he was looking forward to it.

She was to stay at his parents' house the night before, so they didn't see each other before the wedding, a daft idea considering they'd been living in sin for the past two years. 'Living in sin' – what a strange phrase that was. But they both wanted the wedding to be traditional, otherwise they wouldn't be bothering with the whole church ceremony, best man and even a man to give her away. The only thing lacking was a dowry.

"I thought we agreed we'd have no secrets between us," he said solemnly.

"We did and we don't."

That's when she noticed that he held the telephone receiver in his hand. He pressed a button and played back an answerphone message.

Hello, Miss Fisher. My name is Mrs Carlton, from Social Services. I'd be obliged if you would ring me back; I really need to talk to you about your mother, that would be Mrs Shirley Fisher. She has been taken into care this morning and as you are her next of kin, I need you to go over certain matters with me. I hope to hear from you soon. Thank you.

She left a number, but there was no need. It had come up on the caller display.

"You told me your mother was dead," said Ryan. "Do you also have a father out there somewhere?"

She shook her head, wondered whether to lie.

She could tell him she thought her mother was dead, but she didn't want to have to lie to him. The fact was, all these years she had hoped her mother was dead.

"Well?" said Ryan.

"Did I tell you she was dead?" she said obstinately. "Or did you assume?"

"Don't try to wriggle out of it, Ava, please. You know you told me she was dead, or at least that you didn't have a mother. Now Social Services want you to go and talk about her." He paused and sighed deeply. He no longer looked annoyed, only hurt. "How long have we been together?"

"Four years," she replied. She put her arms around his waist to hug him close. "Don't be cross, please. I was raised by my grandmother, from the age of about six. That was twenty years ago and I never saw my mother again, I don't remember her. I don't even know what she looks like, or what she looked like then. When we met, I think I told you I didn't have a mother and that was no lie. I don't."

"I'm not cross," he said. "I just wish you'd told me and I really want to know how she must have hurt you, to make you pretend she was dead."

"She abandoned me. Isn't that enough?"

"Well, she must have you down as her next of

kin or they wouldn't have phoned here. I wonder where they got your phone number from if you've had nothing to do with her in all those years."

"I can't imagine," she said. "It's Social Services; they've got more clout than the police. Anyway, it's too late to phone them now."

"I'll make coffee," he said. "Then you can tell me all about it."

***

"There's not much to tell," said Ava as she struggled with the long strands of spaghetti on her plate. "All I know is that I went to live with my grandmother when I was sixish. When I asked, she always said my mother couldn't cope, that she wasn't well, but later, when I was about twelve, I overheard her telling someone that she had taken me away from her."

She was quiet for a few minutes, so long that Ryan prompted her.

"Is that it?" he asked.

"She wouldn't enlighten me," said Ava. "She only said she had taken me away from my mother because she couldn't cope. She said she had gone round one day and found that I hadn't been washed, my clothes were filthy and I was eating biscuits out of the packet."

"But she didn't get help for your mother, didn't let you see her again?"

Ava shrugged.

"I suppose not. I only know I never saw her again and I don't think she ever asked to see me. I couldn't find anything among my Gran's things when she died, nothing to tell me any more."

"Weren't you curious?" said Ryan. "I would have been. I'd have insisted on going to see her."

"Why? She obviously didn't give a flying wotsit about me, so why should I want to see her?"

"Sounds as though she was mentally ill; *is* mentally ill. If she's been managing alone all these years with no help, you should perhaps have some sympathy for her."

"She hasn't been alone; my father was still with her when I went to live with Gran."

"And he just let your grandmother take you away?"

"He must have, mustn't he? Do you think he cared enough to come and visit?"

He stood up and began to gather the empty plates, scraped the leavings off them and put them in the dishwasher. Ava sipped her second cup of coffee.

"Do you want me to come with you?" he said as he sat down at the table.

"Where?"

"Social Services," he said. "Do you want me to come with you?"

She shook her head.

"I haven't decided yet whether I'm going."

"You have to go," he said. "She's your mother."

Her eyes met his and her mouth turned down. He would never understand, would he? Never in a million years, him with his perfect, lovely mother and his happy childhood. Well, happy until Melanie disappeared anyway. That ruined everything for them and now Ava's mother was going to ruin everything for her and Ryan.

"I wonder why they've taken her into care," he said. "She's too young for Alzheimer's, surely."

"Not necessarily. I've heard it can come early, very early in some cases."

"Well, then. Perhaps she was suffering the first symptoms when your Gran took you to live with her."

Ava knew that wasn't the reason, but she had no idea how she knew or what other reason there could be. All she knew was that whenever her Gran told her how Shirley couldn't cope, Ava had always had the feeling she wasn't being truthful.

"I don't think so, Ryan. I feel nothing for her

and I've always hoped she *was* dead."

The expression on his handsome face was one she had never seen before; it was disapproval and she didn't like it.

"Don't look at me like that," she said. "You can have no idea how I feel about this."

"Probably not, but I know how I'd feel about it."

"Let me decide, Ryan, please," she said. "You don't understand and I doubt I can make you understand. She's never bothered about me and she's not someone I want to call my mother."

CHAPTER TWO

The following morning Ava waited till nine, when she thought the office would be open, then she picked up the phone. She held it for a long time, thinking about that beautiful wedding dress, those lovely pink bridesmaids' dresses, the wonderful wedding they had planned. And as she sat with the phone in her hand, a sense of dread washed over her. Certain that, if she made that call to Mrs Carlton, her wedding plans and all her hopes for the future would be ruined, she dropped the phone back onto the table.

She'd had this time off work to put the last minute touches to the arrangements, not to spend a second of that time concerned about a mother she had never laid eyes on, at least not since she was a small child.

The resentment began to rise; she couldn't help it, could do nothing to suppress it. All her life, whenever she had thought about her mother, she had resented her. That was why she tried not to think about her at all and now she was being forced into it and that only stirred up more resentment.

If there was one thing that infuriated Ava, it was being forced into a position against her will. She had never really known why her mother let her go; Gran hadn't come out and said she had mental health problems, only that she couldn't cope.

Telling Ryan, when they first met, that she had no mother wasn't a lie. She didn't have one, did she? Never had had one. A mother was someone who cared for you, kept you clean and healthy, gave you cuddles and tucked you in at night. A mother was someone who supported you through life, someone who would never part with you no matter what, someone who would fight for you no matter the risk. Above all, a mother was someone who protected you from harm.

No, she didn't have a mother; that was no lie.

Glancing at the clock, Ava realised she'd been sitting here for half an hour, the number she'd copied from the caller display for Mrs Carlton clutched in her hand. Remembering the disapproval in his expression the evening before, she thought it likely that she'd have a similar reaction from this social worker. But she couldn't afford to care. She'd never been one for doing something just because it was expected of her and this was no exception.

She pressed each little button to dial the number on the telephone. Strange, how one still called it 'dialled' even though few telephones had an actual dial nowadays. Only the old fashioned ones had a dial, and there were many people who liked to have an antique looking telephone. Her glance fell on the side table and she wondered how such an antique telephone would look in here.

Her thoughts were still wandering when a voice in her ear startled her by announcing 'Social Services'. She realised she had slouched down into the armchair and she sat up.

"Could I speak to Mrs Carlton, please?" she said.

"I'll see if she's in yet," said the voice on the other end of the line.

Perhaps she won't be, Ava thought. *Then I won't have to speak to her. I've done my bit; I've phoned her back. It's not my fault if she's late for work.*

"Gemma Carlton speaking," said a new voice. *Damn!*

"Ava Fisher," said Ava. "I believe you wanted to speak to me."

"Oh, yes, Miss Fisher. Thank you for getting back to me. I'd really like to come and see you. It's about your mother; I'm afraid she was found wandering along the motorway yesterday morning."

Pity you didn't leave her there. Ava wondered where that had come from. Of course, she didn't know the woman and had no desire to know her, but to wish her dead, squashed under a lorry, was a thought that assailed her without warning.

But when she thought about it, she had in the past had other malicious thoughts about her mother, for no real reason. So, she couldn't cope? There were many things people couldn't cope with; it didn't make them bad people. But there was something, buried deep within Ava's memory, that made her feel nothing but hatred for her mother and she had no idea what that something might be.

"Miss Fisher?" said the voice. "Are you still there?"

"Yes," said Ava. "Sorry, I was thinking. It would really suit me better if I were to come to you."

"Ok, if that's what you'd like. I can free up an hour this afternoon, if that suits."

Why do people always say they could free up time, as though it were chained to something. It was the same as saying they could make time; how the hell do you make time?

"Ok," said Ava. "What time?"

"About 2?"

"Yes, that would be fine. What's the address?"

Gemma told her the address, which she wrote on the same piece of paper as she had written the phone number.

"You'll want the address of the nursing home as well," said Gemma.

"Nursing home?"

"Yes, where they've taken your mother. You'll want to visit her before we meet, won't you?"

"No, I won't," said Ava, then she pressed the red button to disconnect her from Mrs Carlton.

She knew what it must look like, she knew what the social worker would think, but she wasn't *her* mother, was she? And she wasn't Ryan's mother either. No one knew how she felt about the woman and nobody ever could.

***

Ava watched in silence as Mrs Carlton skimmed her eyes over the single sheet of paper in her file. Until asked a question, Ava wasn't about to venture any information of her own, so she sat and wondered why government buildings were all so dreary and depressing.

This place looked exactly like the building Ava had gone to take her driving test. Indeed, she had seen a sign for 'Driving Test Centre' as she drove through this mini-village type complex with its painted white brick walls and grubby blue paintwork. She supposed that at this moment the waiting room was filled with terrified candidates, hoping they could drive well enough for forty minutes or so to be allowed out on the road unaccompanied.

She shifted in her hard, plastic seat.

"Sorry, Miss Fisher," said Mrs Carlton. "I haven't really had much chance to look into this matter; it all happened so suddenly. I can't help wondering why your mother never had a social worker assigned to her."

"Why would she?" asked Ava, causing Mrs Carlton to raise an eyebrow. "I mean, how does an adult come by a social worker? Someone would have had to contact social services, wouldn't they? It's not like children where they're always keeping an eye."

"Well, yes, of course, but obviously she was close enough to dementia or some sort of mental illness for you to be concerned. That sort of thing doesn't come on overnight."

"Doesn't it? I can't say I've ever studied the subject."

"No? That, in itself, is odd. She lived alone, since your father passed?"

Ava shifted again. She hated that phrase 'passed'. If someone had snuffed it, why not bloodywell say so? There was nothing wrong with the word 'died' or 'death'. They were words they used in the Spiritualist Church. They used 'passed' there, or passed over or in spirit, but for practical matters like this, she preferred down to earth expressions. She made no reply and now she could tell that Mrs Carlton was waiting for one.

"Are you saying you didn't notice a change in her?" Gemma persisted.

Here it comes, thought Ava. *Now she'll want to know the ins and outs of why I haven't seen my so-called mother for more than twenty years. Now she'd think I should have sought her out, tried to mend bridges, found out why the old cow abandoned me.*

"Mrs Carlton," Ava said. "I haven't seen my mother since I was six. That was when she turned me over to my grandmother, her mother, and never bothered to visit. You have to excuse me if I don't really care what happens to her. And no, I most certainly wouldn't notice a change in her. In fact, I wouldn't know her if I met her in the street."

Mrs Carlton's eyes widened and her mouth turned down in that disapproving grimace Ava was expecting.

"I see," she said. "Well, you might feel better once you've visited her."

"Feel better than what?"

"Well, obviously she *is* your mother and it's only natural that, now she is older and not in her right mind, you'll want to get to know her. You will probably regret it if you ignore her now."

Ava felt her temper rising. She knew if this conversation went on she'd say something that would never be erased from the social worker's memory. However, in her job she was probably used to that.

"I have only one regret," said Ava. "That is that yesterday I was happy; yesterday I was planning my wedding to the most wonderful man and I was so excited. Yesterday, the most important thing in my mind was that I had finally found the satin shoes I wanted to go with my bridal gown. Then this woman who has nothing to do with me, apart from DNA, apart from that she gave birth to me, rears her ugly head after twenty years and ruins it all. All I need to know now is what you want from me."

The social worker rested her elbows on her desk top, her chin on her knuckles, and studied Ava thoughtfully. She was younger than Ava was expecting, only a few strands of grey in her dark hair and hardly a wrinkle to be seen. That was quite an achievement for someone in a stressful occupation like this.

Finally, she opened her desk drawer and took out a set of keys, which she slid across the wooden desk top towards Ava.

"These are the keys to your mother's house," she said. "You will need to sell it in order to pay for her care."

"Me? Why me?"

"You are all she has."

"And if you hadn't found me, what would happen then?"

Mrs Carlton sighed softly, obviously struggling to keep her disapproval from showing. She was unsuccessful.

"We would sell it, at public sale," she said. "But we wouldn't get nearly so much for it if we auction it off. We'd have to get a house clearance firm in to take everything out and seeing as your mother has lived there for many years and your father passed some years ago, I don't expect the property to be in the best of condition." She paused and shook her head, pursed her lips. "Living alone doesn't suit everybody. She is really not very old to be suffering from dementia, not by today's standards."

Ava bit her lips. *So what are you saying? That I shouldn't have left her alone? That I shouldn't have abandoned her, even though she abandoned me?*

"Why do I care about that?" she said, ignoring Gemma's remarks about her mother living alone. "I mean, obviously you want to get as much as possible for the house, but if you don't, what then? Why is that any concern of mine?"

"At the moment, because she has a house and we needed an emergency placement for her, she is lucky to be in a good home. However, should we not raise enough to cover the costs of such a place, she'll have to move to somewhere not quite so congenial. I shouldn't be telling you that, but it's the way it is and you need to know that."

"Why?"

"To help you realise why you should take the time to clear the house. There's no rush; you have your wedding to think about for now and that must take priority, I see that. But once you've seen her, you might feel you want to make a place for your mother at your wedding."

Just what will it take to get through to this woman?

Ava picked up the keys and pushed back her chair, got to her feet. She wasn't going to argue; she couldn't seem to make the social worker understand that her mother's level of care was of no interest to her. And she had no desire to enter that house.

In fact, she didn't even know where it was.

"Do you have the address?"

"Of the nursing home?" Gemma smiled, showing even white teeth. "Yes, of course."

"Of the house. I need to know where to send the house clearers."

Gemma stopped in the process of writing down the nursing home details on a post- it; she looked as though she was frozen in time for a few seconds, then she frowned, shook her head and wrote down the address of the house as well.

Ava thanked her and left, returned to her car and considered the easiest way to find a genuine, honest, house clearance company.

CHAPTER FOUR

"I've got Monday afternoon off," said Ryan.
"Really?"

She'd been reflecting on how fond she was of Liz and how much different she was from her own mother, or even her grandmother. She'd loved her and cared for her, but there was something missing. Ava supposed it was her age; she came from a generation where parenting was stricter, where a mother was a person to be looked up to and respected, whereas Liz was more of a friend to both her and Ryan.

Ryan had, as always, climbed into bed naked and now Ava slipped off the last of her underwear to join him. She often wondered how couples in love managed in the past, when they had to wait until their wedding night before they could really be together. But even that seemed somehow romantic, to have the anticipation of knowing that they would both be experiencing real, physical love for the first time.

Ava didn't think she could have waited. She loved Ryan far too much, she longed for him and now as his eyes swept over her appreciatively, that little flutter was there, deep inside, telling her that she wanted him now.

She slipped into bed beside him and wrapped her arms round his waist, kissed his nipple then moved her lips up to his to kiss them. Oh, that kiss could warm her whole body, could take her to places she had never imagined before she met him. Because he was the first man she had ever been with, her first and only, also her last. She was sure of that.

He was telling her something, but she couldn't really take it in. Whatever it was, it couldn't be as important as this. He ran his fingers over her skin, took her breast into his mouth and sent her senses into orbit. She wrapped her legs around him, felt his hardness as he took her to heights of ecstasy.

They sighed together and held each other tight.

"Do you think it will still be as good, once we're married?" she asked.

"If I didn't, I'd want to cancel the wedding," he replied with a laugh. "We're meant to be together, Ava. We are a perfect fit, in more ways than one."

She lay in his arms, her head resting on his chest and closed her eyes. Everything else in her life was completely forgotten; all she could think about was of one day very soon being Mrs Ryan Kenyon.

"I said, I have tomorrow afternoon off work," he said.

She snuggled closer, pressed her lips to his chest and felt him stir in response.

"Because?" she said.

"So that I can go with you to visit your mother," he said.

She pushed herself up and stared down at him angrily; he had ruined the moment. But no, it wasn't him, it was that damned woman again. Why on earth couldn't one of those fast drivers on the motorway have hit her? It was obviously what she wanted, taking herself for a stroll along one of the fastest roads in Britain.

"I said I didn't want to visit her," she said.

"I know, but we need to see how ill she is, if she would perhaps enjoy going to the wedding. I understand how you feel but..."

"No!" she interrupted him. "No, you don't understand how I feel and I can never make you understand. Please, Ryan, leave this to me."

She lay back down, but left a gap between them, turned away from him, while he was silent for a long time, so long she thought he had fallen asleep.

But he hadn't.

"I thought we were in this together," he said. "I thought I was your rock, that you were mine. Isn't that what we agreed?"

She turned over, wrapped her arms around him again and held him close.

"Yes, it is, but this is different."

"Then tell me."

"I'm not sure I can," she said. "All I know is that whenever I think about her, I feel so much hatred and resentment, I don't like myself. And I don't ever want you to see that part of me either."

***

It was a beautiful place, an old manor house from Georgian times that had been converted into a care home for the elderly. Thankfully, it hadn't been renamed with any of those cliché titles seen in many of these places and was still called Lawston Manor, after the last Earl Lawston who had been forced to sell the estate to pay for repairs and inheritance taxes.

Ava always found it very sad, that the English nobility had often been forced to sell their estates or open them to the public, or even lease the land to circus kings to open wildlife parks. They were all great to visit, but even so, it diminished the tradition.

Her mind was wandering again. It always did when she was about to be faced with anything unpleasant, and there was nothing so unpleasant in her life right now as her mother.

Now Ava walked slowly toward the main doors, her hand firmly clasped in Ryan's, and tried to calm her racing heart. There were many old ladies and gentlemen in wheelchairs or with walking sticks, even some standing as straight as her. They were sitting on benches, drinking pots of tea outside in the sunshine. None of them were Ava's mother; at least she didn't think so. In truth, she wouldn't know her if she fell over her, so searching the grounds for a familiar face was a complete waste of effort.

Those grounds were beautifully kept, the sort of gardens one might pay to visit. The lawns were expertly trimmed and the flower beds professionally kept; the house itself gave an impression of having taken more than one step back in time. No wonder Mrs Carlton at Social Services was so eager to have the house sold; this place must cost a fortune.

She doesn't deserve it.

Like many of the thoughts she'd had lately, this one came out of nowhere and for no apparent reason, but Ava felt that resentment again, that the mother who had abandoned her, betrayed her, should end her days in such luxury.

Betrayed? She couldn't fathom where that came from. Had she been betrayed? She had no idea, but the word and the notion were quick to show themselves.

The receptionist smiled and led them to a room on the ground floor, overlooking the gardens. It was a large room, large enough for the bed and a full suite of bedroom furniture in light oak. Wardrobe, dressing table, side tables all fitted in with plenty of space and there was a modern en suite bathroom with all the latest fitments.

Looking around, Ava's mind conjured up an image of another bathroom, as vast as this one or even vaster, but there were no modern fittings, just a discoloured and dirty cistern with a rusty pull chain to flush the toilet, an enormous bath, almost deep enough to swim in and big, old fashioned, with rusty taps.

She shuddered and a dart of fear caught at her throat, yet she had no better idea of where this image had come from than she had the resentment and the odd sense of betrayal.

She dredged her memory for any place she might have visited where she could have seen such a sight, and she recalled a sunken bath at a great stately home she had visited once with her grandmother. But it was in no similar condition and she concluded that her memories were mixed, that her mind had confused that sunken bath with a different bathroom and blended them together.

"This is lovely." Ryan's familiar voice penetrated her thoughts. "Isn't it, sweetheart?"

Ava blinked, forced a smile.

"Yes, it's beautiful."

Too good for her. Another thought with a mind of its own and she certainly didn't want Ryan or anyone else to share it.

"Your mother is on the veranda," said the receptionist. "She has her lucid moments, but as the afternoon progresses, they get to be less and less."

She sat looking out over the gardens, the nurse beside her holding her cup with a straw to help her drink. Her hair was completely grey and from what they could see, she was of average build, not too skinny, not too fat. But she looked a lot older than Ava had expected; she wasn't much older than Ryan's mum, but Liz had taken care of herself over the years, even after Melanie vanished. She always said she wanted to look her best when her daughter returned.

They moved around to be seen from Shirley Fisher's front and she stopped drinking and looked up.

"Who are you?" she snapped abruptly.

Ava could not answer. It was almost as though her throat was constricted with fear and she couldn't speak. Her tongue felt swollen, felt as though it was filling her entire mouth.

"This is your daughter, Shirley," said the nurse. "And her fiancé."

The woman called Shirley grimaced, her mouth turned down as though she had seen something unpleasant.

"Not my daughter," she said. "My daughter's at home, where she belongs. She ain't got no bloody fiancé either."

Well, that's fine by me, thought Ava. But that wasn't the only thought that pushed its way into her mind. It was a memory, this one unmuddled and clear, as though it were yesterday.

It's all right; go with your dad. He's your dad; he won't hurt you. I know you don't like that room, but that's just being silly. Nothing wrong with the room. Do as you're told! Go with your dad.

And the voice was familiar. It was the voice she looked to as a child, the voice that told her she was safe. But the voice was as deceitful as its owner, as treacherous as the solace it promised but never delivered.

Ava's eyes filled with tears and she caught back a loud sob before she turned and hurried away, picking up speed until she was running, back toward those main doors, leaving Ryan still observing the woman they said was her mother.

***

Ava had no idea how long she sat there, hunched up and shaking, on one of those benches in the grounds, before she felt a comforting arm around her, a soothing kiss on her cheek, felt herself being pulled into the arms of this man who meant so much to her. Yet now she could feel herself being pulled away from him by a past she had forgotten, a past she had buried with her childhood.

"She didn't mean it," he said.

"Yes, she did," said Ava.

"She's senile. She doesn't know what she's saying."

"I don't care, Ryan." She sat up straight, reached into her handbag for a tissue and wiped her face. "I haven't had anything to do with her since I was a little child; I couldn't even remember what she looked like. She was never a part of my life and now she's back, and she's going to destroy everything."

"All right," he said. He looked about thoughtfully, considering the other residents seated about the grounds. "They all look happy enough and well cared for. It's a nice place, expensive I should think."

"That's what the social worker said."

"We'll get the house cleared out and sold. It shouldn't take long, even in the state it's in, not in that area. All you really want is to make sure she's cared for."

I don't care how well she's cared for, thought Ava. *I don't care if she starves to death.*

Then she remembered something else. She remembered how she could never stand to be hungry, how she had to head straight for the nearest restaurant or sandwich bar the minute that little ache came on. The panic would set in if that hunger were not satisfied straight away. She was lucky to have the sort of metabolism that kept her slim.

You'll stay in here and you'll get nothing to eat till you do as you're told. It was that room, that same room that she hated so much, the room with the sunken bath, the bath that was deep enough to swim in.

"Let's go, Ryan," she said, getting to her feet. "I didn't want to come here and I certainly don't want to stay."

"The nurse said she's more lucid in the morning. Perhaps we should come back then, at the weekend."

"No. I've seen all I want to see."

"But..."

"No buts, please. You don't understand; I've said it before."

"You obviously have bad memories," he said. "I wish you'd share them with me."

"I can't."

"You can; you can tell me anything, you know that."

They'd arrived at his car and now she turned to face him across the vehicle, her hand on the door handle, holding the half open door.

"Not this. I can't share the memories, because I can't remember them. I only know they are there and they are cruel."

***

Only a few days now to the wedding. Everything was done, no more last minute details. She'd seen to the caterer, seen the florist and got further reassurance that her gold roses would be there in time. The dressmakers had long ago finished putting the finishing touches to the wedding gown and the bridesmaids' dresses. They were pink because that was Melanie's favourite colour. Ryan had asked her to do that; she was going to have lavender, but it was an easy concession to make. It was his wedding, too. The cars were booked. She had phoned the car hire place that very morning, for the third time and she could hear the patient little sigh the owner tried to hide.

She began to wish she had never asked for two weeks off work before the big day; one would have done. She switched on the television, something she never did in the mornings, and found one of those awful programmes where people air their private lives in public, where the host arranges DNA tests to be sure the man was, indeed, the father of the woman's baby.

She switched it off and made herself a second cup of tea. As she waited for the kettle to boil, her eyes wandered to the hooks on the wall where hung the keys to the house in Dog Kennel Lane. Like a magnet, they seemed to draw her to them, despite her promise to herself to ignore the place until after the honeymoon.

She had nothing else to do. Television was abysmal and watching a DVD at this time of day just seemed somehow decadent. Time enough for that when she got as old and infirm as some of those people at Lawston Manor.

She could go and have a look at the house, couldn't she? There was no harm in that. She could go and see what state the place was in; she couldn't rely on the internet for it, could she? That picture could be years old. It might have been done up since then.

Still, she had no code or keys to the front gates. They looked electronic, so she'd need an access code or a fob and she had neither. It might be that she couldn't open them, wouldn't be able to get in.

That thought brought with it a small ray of hope and she fought it back. If she didn't want to go and see the house, she didn't have to. Why wait for an excuse to stay away, to get locked out?

I won't go. It'll wait till after the honeymoon. It'll wait full stop; let house clearers and estate agents do it.

But Ryan didn't want her to do that; he thought it was odd, weird even to not want to look around, perhaps find important documents, even discover just why her grandmother had taken her away, raised her herself. She couldn't make him see why she didn't want to do that, because she didn't know herself. She couldn't admit that she didn't want to ask those questions because she didn't want the answers. The thought of those answers terrified her and she didn't want to know them. She would have to do it, but it could wait.

She'd read the newspaper, try the television again, or perhaps wander round the shops. But she hated going round shops without enough money to buy what she wanted and the wedding had cost so much, she had to be careful.

She made her tea and sat down to drink it at the kitchen table, beside the window which overlooked the garden. They'd made it pretty and in the summer, the flowers produced beautiful colour. She loved their little house; it could not be more different from that place at the end of Dog Kennel Lane, that house in which she was born and for which, for some unknown reason, she felt nothing but fear and dread.

Finally, she drained her cup and picked up the keys. She wouldn't be able to get in; the gates would be locked and she didn't have the code. She knew that, she hoped that.

At least she could say she'd tried.

***

It didn't take long to get to the house. Primrose Cottage, it was called, although it couldn't be less like a cottage if it tried. Or a primrose.

Ava turned into Dog Kennel Lane and drove slowly, as slowly as she could, passed the sign which told her this was a private road. There was nothing behind her, no vehicle following so she was holding no one up, and she wanted to get a good look at the other houses.

They were all large, palatial semi-mansions, all with electronic gates, some wrought iron, others oak. Behind those gates were lush front gardens, trees and shrubs showing their tops above the high fences.

Every house had a name, mostly a name that ended with 'Lodge' or 'House' or simply 'Cottage' like Primrose Cottage, like the one to which Ava had the keys, lying on the passenger seat where she had thrown them.

She was going so slow, she was able to spare quick glances at her surroundings and she could not help but notice the twitching curtains, the quickly moving shutters, even an open upstairs window with a face full of curiosity peering from it.

In the driveways of these houses, the ones she could see anyway, were very expensive cars, prestige models, all new or nearly new. At least Ava's car wouldn't attract attention; it was last year's model BMW five series in metallic sky blue.

She hadn't bothered to dress up, still wore her jeans and a jumper, new, although from a budget store. She never could see the point of paying a fortune for casual clothes, even if she could afford to. But right now she couldn't, not after the expensive wedding and the planned honeymoon.

She drew nearer, got to the very end of the road and turned the car before coming to a stop outside. There were a lot of trees between the house and the outer fence, on both sides, so the building itself was a long way from all the other houses.

She sat and stared at the house for a long time, just to be sure. Sure of what she couldn't have said. At last, she picked up the keys and got out of the car, pressed the remote to lock it and took a few, diffident steps toward the rusty, wrought iron gates.

That's when she saw that the gates were not locked. There was a gap between them, just a small one, but one gentle push was enough to open them wider. The gate creaked, got stuck on the gravel surface beneath. It wasn't wide enough for a car, but for someone on foot, it offered easy access.

She pushed the other gate and it did the same, creaked loudly, got stuck on the gravel beneath it. She didn't think it would be too difficult to scrape the driveway so the gates opened wide, but for now she stood, just inside them and stared up at the ramshackle house.

It was large, just as enormous as the other houses in the road if not more so, but that's where the similarity ended. It had wooden slates which had once been white, but now they were covered in dirt and moss, the paint peeling.

The sign that declared this to be 'Primrose Cottage' was hanging from one nail, its wood rotting, its paint peeling. It looked as if it had once been a bright primrose yellow colour with brownish writing, but not any more. Now it was fit for nothing but the bonfire.

Two of the windows were cracked and the balcony outside one of the rooms on the upper storey had collapsed. The floor had caved in and was hanging over the driveway below.

Ava didn't move, didn't venture any further inside the property. That constriction of her throat was back again as a lump formed, and she realised that her teeth were chattering. It wasn't cold, wasn't even cool, but still her teeth clattered together and she couldn't stop them. She shivered, began to shake, her stomach churned and her bladder relaxed a little. She turned and ran back to her car.

"Excuse me," said an unfamiliar female voice.

Ava turned to see a tall woman approaching her, her blonde curls perfectly styled. She was probably in her fifties, although she fought hard to disguise the fact, and she was dressed expensively, very expensively, in clothes Ava had only thought about.

"Yes," she replied tersely.

She managed to pull herself together, control her treacherous body which was about to give her away, reveal her terror.

Ava clutched her car keys in one hand, the keys to Primrose Cottage in the other, and wished the woman would go away.

"Do you have authority to be here?" said the stranger, whom Ava assumed was a neighbour, a nosy neighbour. She drew a deep breath.

"Do you have authority to ask that question?" said Ava.

The neighbour took a step back, her cheeks flushed.

"I live at Marigold Lodge," she replied. She offered a handshake which Ava felt obliged to accept. "Cheryl Bradley," she went on. "I saw the car, saw you and with the gates broken, I thought it best to see who it was. Once it gets about that a house like this is empty, certain elements from the lower part of town find their way here, hoping to discover valuables."

"Is that right?" said Ava. "Well, I'm not an element from the lower part of town and everything in that house rightfully belongs to me, so you needn't worry. I'll probably get the gates fixed as soon as possible."

"Oh, you're a relative then?" said Cheryl. "I didn't know she had any."

"I'm not surprised."

"I heard she was found wandering the motorway," said Cheryl. "I didn't know she was senile."

"Is there a reason why you should?"

Ava was getting angry now. It was obvious to her that this woman wanted only to find out details about her mother, about the house and what would happen to it. It seemed she didn't even know the owner's name, much less anything about her.

"She was a recluse," said Cheryl, drawing herself up indignantly. "A few of the residents here tried on several occasions to check on her wellbeing, but she refused to answer the door." She paused, waiting for a response, but Ava had none to give her. "When she was a bit younger she'd come out occasionally, but she was too taciturn and volatile; we all thought she could be violent."

Ava was beginning to get even more irritated with this woman. Her upper class accent was so obviously faked; Ava was tempted to tell her so. If you're going to have pretensions to a posh accent, don't use long words that don't belong. That always gave you away, even if nothing else did.

"Will she be going into a care home now?" said Cheryl.

Mind your own business, was what Ava was tempted to reply, but her grandmother had raised her to be more polite than that. She wasn't quite that irritated yet.

"I expect so," she replied. "The house will be sold, once I've had it cleared out. You'll have to excuse me; I'm in a bit of a rush."

She moved toward her car again, pointed the remote at it and clicked the button, but she wasn't to be allowed to get any farther.

"You didn't tell me your name," said Cheryl.

No, I didn't, did I?

"Fisher," she said. "Ava Fisher."

That was enough. She was going to get into her car and drive away, and nobody was going to stop her, not this time. She opened the car door, glanced up at the house again and felt that sinking feeling in her stomach sweep over her once more. She wasn't about to tell this woman anything more, no matter how ill mannered she might seem.

"And..." Cheryl began, but Ava slipped into the driver's seat and closed the door.

"I have to go," she said and she drove away, glad she had thought to turn the car around when she arrived.

Checking the rear view mirror as her turning came into view, she saw that Cheryl was still standing outside the house; then she held up a mobile phone and took a photograph of Ava's car. Ava smiled.

Just in case I'm one of those elements from the lower end of town.

***

After lunch she watched a film on television

and wondered how anyone coped with being at home all day. She tried to read a book, but with the wedding on Saturday, and this business with the house and a mother she'd rather forget, she knew she wouldn't be able to concentrate.

As she was at home, she might as well make something complicated for dinner. She went online to look for recipes but ended thinking she'd just make lasagne instead. There were lots of recipes, but none she thought Ryan would like. He was a fussy sod when it came to food, wouldn't even eat Chinese and she wanted everything to go smoothly. She knew he'd be asking about the house, wanting to know if she'd been there, what she had found inside, wanting to know why she hadn't *been* inside.

She didn't know that herself. She only knew the shroud of doom that engulfed her whenever she thought about it.

CHAPTER THREE

Ava took one glance at the address on the note, noted the unusual name of the street, then stuffed it into the pocket of her trousers. She had an appointment with the florist this morning, then she needed to be sure the caterers had managed to acquire all the food she'd requested. She had to visit the confectioners who were making the chocolate fountain for the reception. Then there was the saxophonist, who needed a deposit to buy a suitable dress to wear.

Ava had heard her by chance, busking on the street for coins, and asked her to play at the reception. She was brilliant, very talented and just what Ava was hoping for.

By the time she had done all that, it was getting too late to worry about the house in Dog Kennel Lane. She drove home and put a chicken in the oven, peeled some potatoes ready for boiling and set the table.

Dog Kennel Lane; it sounded like the most awful place, one of those estates with houses nobody gave a monkey's wotsit about.

Ryan would be home in about an hour and she wanted to look up a house clearance place before he arrived. She'd sensed last night that he, too, would never understand how she felt, just like that social worker. She didn't want him interfering, telling her she should see what secrets were to be found hidden in the house.

Then she felt guilty for thinking like that. She loved Ryan, loved him more than she had ever loved anyone in her entire life, and loving anyone had never been easy for her. She'd had a dog once whom she loved, but then her trust in animals was always greater than her trust in humans. Her own mother hadn't wanted her, so how could she expect anyone else to? It was odd how she never included her father in that condemnation. He could not have wanted her either, could he? Otherwise he'd have stopped Gran from taking her.

There was something frightening about her memories of him, although she couldn't have said what. She didn't even remember what he looked like; she only knew that thinking about him brought a shudder.

When she met Ryan she had fallen head over heels, as they say. She knew that, provided she was honest, he would support her. But she didn't feel like being honest, not about this. This was a secret she had kept buried her entire life and she couldn't reveal it to anyone, not even Ryan. Not even herself, if she were honest. For the secret she had hidden deep within her mind was a secret that refused to reveal itself, even to her.

She looked up the address on Google Earth. Lord knows why, except that she might need to tell the house clearance people where it was. What she found was a large, detached, clapboard house, the once white wood now black and with dark green moss growing in between the slats.

It was huge and it had a large front driveway for cars, although there were none there on this film, and there were double, wrought iron gates which seemed to be electronic. She glanced again at the note bearing the address; no, there was no code to open the gates. She thought perhaps the security part no longer worked.

As she moved the screen around, she discovered that Dog Kennel Lane was not the run down area such a title might infer; it was, in fact, a very expensive area, full of wealthy looking houses which backed onto to the many acres of a public heath, where people could be seen walking their dogs.

Ava zoomed the image in as close as it would go. The house had two brick pillars and a plaque with a name, too far away to be deciphered on the screen; perhaps when she got to the house, it would be clearer. *Got to the house? What am I thinking?* She shook her head.

It had an enormous garden, must have been

three or four acres, and it seemed to be tucked away at the very end of a cul-de-sac, far from the other houses, and judging by the state of it, Ava thought the neighbours would be happy about that. They would also be happy to see it sold.

There seemed to be a lot of trees to the sides and at the very end of the garden, taking up about half the space. And there was a swing; it could barely be seen on the laptop screen, but a vague memory leapt out at her when she looked at it. It was that of a little girl, swinging happily, screaming with excitement, and being pushed by a man, though she could not drag up an image of him.

She'd been so engrossed, she hadn't heard the door open, only knew that Ryan was home when she felt his touch on her shoulder, his kiss on her cheek.

"Thinking of buying?" he said.

"Not this, no," she answered, too quickly.

"That's a relief. Dog Kennel Lane is very expensive, out of our price range. Perhaps one day. Anyway, that one doesn't look too healthy."

"It certainly doesn't."

She aimed the cursor at the little cross on the corner of the screen to make the Google Earth image go away, but Ryan held her wrist to stop her.

"Why are you looking?" he asked.

There was no way out now, no good excuse for looking at a run down house in a posh avenue.

"It's my mother's house," she said quietly.

"Really? It's probably worth a few hundred thousand, even if it is in a state."

Finally, she managed to click on that little cross, forgetting that the window beneath it was a house clearance firm.

"What's this for?" asked Ryan.

He straightened up and went to the kitchen, put the potatoes on to boil and made tea for them both. She followed him.

"Sorry," he said, handing her a steaming mug. "I didn't ask how the meeting went. Obviously, you learned something."

"It was okay," she said. They sat on the sofa while they waited for the dinner to be ready. "She said I've got to sell the house to pay for the care home."

"Well, tomorrow's Saturday. We can go and have a look."

"I'm busy tomorrow. I need to see to some last minute details for the wedding and Sunday we're going to your mum's for dinner. She's expecting us. The social worker said it would wait."

"She might be able to wait," he said. "I'm not

sure I can."

She bit her lips thoughtfully. It was a habit of hers, one Ryan had remarked on before. He reckoned she'd put her lips out of shape if she didn't stop doing it.

"They're beautiful lips," he said now, not for the first time. "You don't want to spoil them."

She used them now, putting her tea down on a side table and moving close to kiss him. It was a long, lingering kiss, the sort of kiss that sent a quiver of anticipation through her body. As soon as dinner was eaten, she knew precisely what she was going to do and it had nothing to do with her mother or her run down old house.

***

"If you give me the address," said Ryan over breakfast the following morning, "I'll go and have a look, as you're busy today."

No! The word screamed silently at her, but she had no idea why or where it came from. What was wrong with Ryan going to the house? She didn't know, but she knew she didn't want him to.

Before she looked at the house on Google Earth, she thought it was totally unfamiliar, but for some reason, she had a faint memory of the place and it wasn't a memory that brought with it a feeling of comfort and security. It was daft; she hadn't been there since she was a child. She could remember nothing about the place, or about her parents, but something in the image made her want to run away and hide.

She only knew she didn't want Ryan tainted with it, didn't want him contaminated by being anywhere near it.

"Ryan, I'd really rather leave it alone until after the wedding. We've got air tickets to Florida; they cost a fortune. You don't want anything to spoil our trip, do you?"

He leaned across the table and gently touched her lips with his own. That was one of the things she loved about Ryan, the way he showed little signs of affection for no apparent reason. A little flutter deep down tempted her to forget today and go back to bed, but she really did have appointments lined up.

"You're right, of course," he said. "But I insist on going with you when you visit her."

"Visit who?"

"Who do you think? Your mother."

Visit her? She had no intention of visiting her, not now, not ever. But the sudden realisation that she might not be able to avoid it sent her into a depression. Now her day was spoilt and she needed to get to the florist, if only to cheer herself up.

The following day they arrived at the home of Ryan's mother, a place Ava always found warm and comforting. It was a second home to her now, since her grandmother died and the money from her house had paid for their brand new one and gone a good way toward the wedding. They were lucky, to be starting out without a mortgage to pay and a bit of spare cash. *Thank you, Gran.*

Ava would give it all back to have Gran see her married, though, and now she felt sad to be thinking about her. She knew that her Gran would see it, that she'd be looking down on them on their special day. Ava wanted to tell Liz that her little Melanie would also be looking down on her brother on his wedding day, but she was afraid of how she might take it. Some people thought any mention of a spirit world to be a scam. Besides, Liz had never admitted that Melanie was dead and still clung to a hopeless and forlorn belief that she might still be alive somewhere.

Now they hugged Liz and made their way into the lounge, the tempting aroma of roasting meat making their stomachs rumble. Liz was a wonderful cook and she enjoyed having her son and his fiancée come for dinner, as she loved to have Ryan to fuss over once in a while.

Everywhere Ava looked there were

photographs of Melanie, some with Ryan, some on her own. They were on the mantelpiece, on the bookcase, on the coffee tables and there was a huge oil portrait hanging on the wall.

She was a pretty little thing. Bright blonde curls framed a round, face with soft skin and a happy smile. In her hair was a pink ribbon, matching her hand knitted cardigan, and Ava wanted to hold her in her arms.

The photographs stopped when Melanie got to be seven years old. There were lots before that, but none after, for that was when she disappeared, snatched from her bicycle one bright, summer day and never seen again.

They found the bike; they never found Melanie. But the police never closed a case involving a missing child and despite extensive searches, they still acted on any new lead.

Ryan was five years older than his little sister and he felt responsible, although he wasn't even there when it happened. He thought he ought to have been looking after her.

"Dinner's nearly ready," Liz called from the kitchen. "Be about five minutes. Make yourselves at home."

Ava leaned closer to Ryan and kept her voice low.

"I wonder what you'd think if, when we've got the wedding pictures back, we had Melanie added. I know someone at work who's really good with that sort of thing and she could probably put her in a bridesmaid dress as well." She paused to watch his expression, but it didn't change; he looked the same, only thoughtful. "What do you think? Would your mum like that, or would it upset her?"

He smiled, that gorgeous smile she could never resist.

"I don't know," he said. "I'll have to think about it."

She nodded. For her own part, she could never understand how Liz could bear to see all those photographs everywhere, but not being a mother, she probably wouldn't. Different people dealt with grief in different ways and she supposed they gave her comfort.

In one of the pictures of Melanie with Ryan, he was sitting and she had her arm hanging over her brother's shoulder, both smiling happily. That one was taken just a week before Melanie disappeared, when they both thought they had a future.

Ryan had never really got over losing his sister. They were obviously really close; she was his best friend, his playmate and he'd never forgiven himself for not being with her that day. Ava knew it still hurt him and that he would always blame himself.

Usually, Liz spoke mostly about her missing daughter, but now she had something else to think about and that was her son's wedding. Having no mother of her own, Ava was planning on being sure Liz had pride of place.

"Everything's organised," Ava said. "All we need now is some sunshine."

"I'm really looking forward to it," said Liz. "Tell me, Ava, do you think Melanie is looking down on us?"

Ava stiffened. This was something she'd wanted to discuss with her, but she was unprepared for the abruptness of the question.

"I'm quite sure she will be, along with my grandmother. Perhaps they'll be there together."

"And your mother," said Liz.

Silence followed her remark, complete and uncomfortable. Then Ryan spoke up, without asking Ava, without asking anyone.

"Ava's mother is still alive, Mum," he said.

Liz stared at her, her frown full of suspicion, but she obviously had no idea what to say.

"I don't understand," she said at last. "You said she was dead."

She was. It was tempting to say it and it was what Ava wanted to say. She was dead and now she's alive and spoiling everything. Quickly, she collected her thoughts.

"I'm sorry, Liz, but until very recently I

thought she was," she said.

She squeezed Ryan's hand, hoping he wouldn't contradict her, but she said no more. What more was there to say? No, she didn't believe she was dead, just hoped she was, when she'd thought about her at all. But Liz wasn't prepared to leave it there.

"You thought she was dead?" she said. "Did your grandmother tell you that?"

"Sort of. I can't remember her saying it in so many words, but it's what I always assumed."

"And now you know different? How wonderful."

"I wouldn't call it that," said Ava.

"Have you told the caterers?"

What the hell has it got to do with them?

Ava was beginning to feel twisted and tied up in all these questions. Did nobody understand why she had no desire to know this so-called mother?

"She won't be coming to the wedding," Ava said abruptly.

"Oh, but she must," said Liz.

"No. She is demented, was found wandering the motorway in the middle of the night."

Pity the drivers were so careful. She wondered where the vicious thought had come from. She didn't know this woman! Why should she hate her so much?

"I'm sure something can be arranged," said Ryan. "Perhaps the nursing home can send a carer with her, or perhaps we can hire someone for the day. We'll sort it out."

Ava made no reply. She wanted to scream, she wanted to cry, she wanted to hit them both, tell them to mind their own business. And she had no idea why.

"She has a house on the other side of town," Ryan told his mother. "Ava has to sell it to pay for her care. It's in a place called Dog Kennel Lane."

"Oh, I know that," said Liz. "It's very upmarket."

"That's what I thought," said Ryan. "Do you know why it's called Dog Kennel Lane?"

"Yes, I do. A few centuries ago one of the Kings had his hunting dogs kennelled there."

"Ah, I wondered where it got such an odd name. Do you know which King?"

"I don't, I'm afraid," said Liz. "I'm not really up on history, but I can find out."

"That'll be really interesting," said Ryan, then he turned to Ava. "Won't it?"

Ava took a deep breath to steady her rising temper.

"I might not have to sell it," she said. "They don't really know if she's got early onset Alzheimer's or whether she is mentally ill. If she is, it might be curable and she'll be able to go home."

The idea had come out of nowhere, out of her hope that she might never have to go near the house.

"You didn't tell me that," said Ryan.

"Didn't I? Sorry, darling. There's just been more important things going on."

More important? I shouldn't have said that. Now he'll think me callous.

But they were more important. Her wedding and her future with Ryan was far more important than a mother who had abandoned her, a woman she didn't want to know and her ramshackle old house.

Still trying to suppress the resentment that was forcing its way into her mind, she wished her grandmother was here to tell her why she felt so much hatred for a mother she couldn't remember.

CHAPTER FIVE

Ava discovered that it was not possible to force a worry out of her mind, not completely. But she did manage to hide it behind the exciting things that were going to happen to her that day.

The sun's rays streamed through her windows and she rolled out of bed and pulled open the curtains. There wasn't a cloud to be seen, but she could see the trees bending in the breeze. This was just what she'd hoped for and she had no intention of allowing Primrose Cottage and her crazy mother to spoil things.

There was her beautiful gown with its lace bodice tapering into a full skirt with many layers. There was her wonderful headdress, made of flowers with a long, delicate veil cascading from it.

Today she would belong to Ryan, in mind, body and soul and he would belong to her. She would take his name, be entitled to call herself 'Mrs' and be his wife. That was a title she had wanted for herself almost from the moment she met him. 'Wife'.

Many couples their age now rejected the idea of marriage altogether. It wasn't like the days when a woman couldn't even be left alone in the same room as a man without some evil minded old hag thinking there was something wrong, something immoral going on.

Ava recalled her grandmother, talking about a girl Ava had gone to school with who had moved into a flat with her boyfriend. She remembered how she'd told Ava that now she was 'damaged goods' and no one else would want her.

Apparently, her boyfriend wouldn't want her for long either, not now she had given in to him before marriage. He'd lose respect.

Gran was long gone when Ava met Ryan, and she often wondered what she would think of them living together. Some of Ava's friends had children now, but were still not married and had no intention of ever being so. It was only a piece of paper, they said, but Ava had always wanted to be the wife of the man she loved. And she loved Ryan.

This room had been Ryan's before he had moved in with Ava. Liz hadn't redecorated it, or changed anything. Ava supposed she had kept it the same in case things didn't work out and he wanted to move back in. She tried to understand, although it pulled at her heart to think about it. If she were a mother, she might do the same, but until she was a mother, she wouldn't really know.

She'd stayed there last night, in his bed, so

they wouldn't meet before the wedding. It was a tradition going back centuries, back to the days when the bride and groom had never met at all before they married. It was all arranged by their parents and sometimes they were still children.

Now Ava sat on the bed and looked around the room of an older teenage boy or perhaps a young, single man. Over on the other wall was an enormous poster of Marilyn Monroe, the one where she was standing on an air vent and her skirt was blowing up, showing her bare legs and her knickers. Back when the photograph was taken, men drooled over it, thought it was really risqué. It was kind of sweet, quaint even, but Ava was glad those days were long gone.

Then there were the football scarves and masculine black wallpaper. Beside Monroe was a picture of Melanie and Ryan with their arms around each other. It was blown up to be almost as big as the poster, and they both looked so happy. Melanie was smiling, laughing just like Marilyn in that famous photograph.

It was a winter photo, one with snow in the background and just the edge of a big snowman. Melanie was wearing a thick, hand knitted bobble hat and her chin was snuggled into a matching scarf. Liz had made that set and she told Ava that she had given up knitting since she no longer had a little girl to knit for.

Twelve years since she vanished, and there had been no sign of her. The trail had gone cold, such as it was, which wasn't much. Several children had disappeared during those years and the police assumed Melanie had gone the same way as them, although they never actually came out and said so. But she was the last; no more little girls had gone missing after Melanie. That could have been nothing more than parents keeping a closer eye on their children; Ava didn't suppose they would ever know.

If Melanie walked in now, it would put the icing on the cake of this day, it really would.

For the first time Ava felt as though she were a real part of this family. It might have been staying overnight in this room full of Ryan, it might have been knowing that today she would share their name, but for the first time she felt a kinship with Melanie, felt that pull on her heartstrings, felt the worry and the anguish of not knowing for certain what had happened to her.

Attached to her bouquet, Ava had a small picture of Melanie. Ryan had suggested it and she was happy to agree, and in the reception hall, as guests arrived, they would be faced with a big picture of the little girl, enhanced with a dress to match the bridesmaids.

She'd be nineteen now, old enough to join the

adult bridesmaids, old enough even to be the maid of honour, but she had never grown older than the laughing little girl in the snow.

Ava's friends arrived to help her with her make up and her hair, then they all helped each other with their dresses and their own make up and hair before they helped Ava on with her wonderful gown. She sat on the bed to slip her feet into those delicate satin shoes that had taken her so long to find. The bridesmaids had silver sandals, too high for Ava as she was almost as tall as Ryan anyway. She certainly didn't want to walk beside him and be taller than him; that would never do.

Everything went to plan. The cars, beautiful white Rolls Royces, arrived on time, Ava walked, her arm linked into that of Ryan's father, down the aisle to the altar where waited the love of her life.

Her heart ached with the joy of it, her eyes filled with tears and she heard little of the service, only responded automatically as she spoke her vows. There would be no writing their own vows, not in Ava's wedding ceremony. She wanted this to be as traditional as possible. The only thing left out was the promise to obey; they both thought that too antiquated and offensive to women to even consider. But everything else was in place.

At the end, the vicar pronounced them husband and wife and Ava fell into Ryan's arms, kissed him fervently, a little too fervently for public display, so he whispered to her. But she was so happy, she couldn't express it any other way.

The reception was wonderful and they left their guests to it to drive to the airport and catch their flight. Ryan had a surprise waiting for her there; he had upgraded their tickets to first class.

"How can we afford that?" she said.

"I told the airline it was our honeymoon and I was promised that, if there were any first class seats left when they took off, we could have them for no extra charge."

"Seriously?" He nodded. "That was so good of them. We must let everyone know."

They settled into seats that were like armchairs and he leaned across and kissed her.

"Are you happy?"

"Oh, yes," she said. "I couldn't be happier."

She rested her head on his shoulder and closed her eyes, then that thought that she had pushed away reared its ugliness.

Please don't spoil it. Please don't start asking when I'm going to clear out the bloody house.

But he didn't. He only closed his eyes and settled down, her hand clasped firmly in his. He lifted that hand to his lips and kissed it and waited until they had taken off and soared over the patchwork of English fields before he switched on the television sets to watch a film.

Appropriately, it was a love story, a romance; a happy ending guaranteed.

***

Florida was just as Ava had imagined. She had always wanted to go there, but Gran said they couldn't afford it and she had never been on an aeroplane. She was frightened of the idea and wouldn't know how to go about getting a passport and finding the right plane. Then there was the problem of getting a passport for Ava. As a child, she would need permission from either her mother or her father, and that meant going back to Primrose Cottage and asking Shirley. It wasn't worth the risk and now Ava understood her reluctance perfectly.

They stayed at one of the Disney hotels and hired a car to get to the other parks and the coast. They took turns in driving; neither had ever driven on the right before and it was a bit scary, but they soon got used to it.

After the first few days, Ava stopped worrying that Ryan might bring up the subject of the house, the mother or the nursing home. She could comfortably forget about them, at least until they landed back at Heathrow.

She'd had a few worries, even before the mother thing reared its ugly head. One had been that being married might take the romance out of their relationship. Of course, they'd only had the honeymoon so far, but something had happened she would never have believed possible - she loved him even more than she ever had. They'd made love every night and each time had been better than the last.

As the plane landed to a typical rainy morning in London, Ava found herself silently thanking Gran for leaving her house to her so that they could sell it and buy their own newer house, as well as pay for this glorious trip.

She forgot to leave a warm jacket out of her luggage, stupidly expecting the same sunshine they had left behind half way across the world. Now she shivered as they approached Ryan's car in the multi storey car park that had taken them at least fifteen minutes to walk to, pushing the trolley loaded with their bags and souvenirs before them.

Ryan's remote opened the boot and he pulled out the heavy jacket that he always kept there in case he broke down. He wrapped it around Ava and began to fit the cases and bags inside, while she almost ran to open the passenger door and jump inside the car. Ryan had the keys, so she couldn't start the engine, which in turn meant she couldn't switch on the heater, so all she could do was snuggle down into the enormous jacket.

As he got into the car, he took from his pocket a small, gift wrapped box. Then he slid into the driver's seat and started the engine himself. It didn't take long to warm up before the heater could be got going, then he leaned across and kissed her, handed her the box.

More? She thought. *After that fabulous wedding, that wondrous honeymoon, surely there could be no more.*

"What's this?" she asked.

"It's for my mother, to thank her for all her hard work," he said.

Her heart sank, but then she felt very selfish. Of course Liz deserved a nice present; she'd practically organised the whole thing for them. But she hoped he wasn't going to be one of those men who still clung to his mother. She'd had a friend from school whose marriage fell apart after only two years for that very reason.

"What is it?" she asked.

"Just some pearls." He stopped for a red traffic light, reached into the pocket of the jacket Ava wore and took out another, gift wrapped box. He tossed it into her lap. "Pearls wouldn't suit you. You're much too young."

Inside the box were some beautiful diamond earrings. He must have bought them before they left London and hid them in the pocket of his emergency jacket while they went on their honeymoon.

Her heart swelled. She was so lucky, so very fortunate to have found this man.

When she first met Ryan, she was reluctant to commit to a relationship. Something made her fearful of the idea of being with a man, being physically with a man. She couldn't have said what. She scarcely remembered her grandfather, so it wasn't anything he had done. Now she knew about Primrose Cottage, she recognised the feeling she'd had about it; it was that same cloud of dread that hovered over her when she looked at the place, when she thought about putting one step inside.

She had been wrong about Ryan. Perhaps she was also wrong about Primrose Cottage.

CHAPTER SIX

Ava had another week after Ryan had to return to work. He was a software engineer and head of the department; some of the projects they were working on couldn't go forward without him.

Ava worked in the advertising department of a local newspaper and she was owed holiday time. She had planned to re-arrange the house to accommodate the new things they'd been given as wedding presents.

The decorators had been in whilst they'd been away and she couldn't stop admiring the beautiful new silver and grey wallpaper and white paintwork. They'd done a great job and they were trustworthy. She'd given an extra key to the next door neighbour in case of problems, but there hadn't been any. She made a mental note to keep the decorators' number for future reference and to recommend them to her friends.

She felt happy for a couple of hours or so, that first day. She was missing Ryan, having had him with her constantly for the last two weeks, but she expected that to wear off once she returned to her own job.

She had switched on the radio, just for the noise, and was making a list of all the things she wanted to get on with when the phone rang. Putting her list aside, she pushed herself up from the sofa and went to answer it; it could be one of her friends, or it might be Liz. It might even be Ryan, missing her as much as she missed him. That was a notion to bring a smile to her face.

But the smile turned to a grim line of disappointment and irritation when she heard the voice on the other end of the line.

"It's Mrs Carlton here, from Social Services," said the voice. "Am I speaking to Miss Fisher?"

"No. You are speaking to Mrs Kenyon."

"Forgive me," said Mrs Carlton. "I forgot you had been away on your honeymoon, not simply a holiday. Did you have a good time?"

I did until you phoned.

"We did, thank you," replied Ava. "There's still a little jet lag, but nothing too traumatic."

Silence was her only reply, a silence that lasted some few seconds, almost a minute. Ava guessed the social worker was waiting for her to enquire after the health of her mother; she had no interest in such a thing and had no intention of asking. At last Mrs Carlton spoke.

"I wondered if you'd given any further thought to your mother's house," she said. "I'm told the doctors are confident now that she'll never be safe to live alone again. It seems likely that it is early onset Alzheimer's." She paused, waiting, but Ava made no reply. "Expenses are adding up and the nursing home gets no government grant, you know."

"Doesn't it?" said Ava. "Why didn't you put her in one that was state funded, then?"

She could hear Mrs Carlton's disapproval at the end of the line. There was no particular sound, not one that could be easily discerned, but she could hear it just the same.

"We accommodated your mother in the only place available at the time," she replied. "But let me assure you, *Mrs* Kenyon that even if she occupied a bed in the cheapest place available, she would still need to pay from the proceeds of her house."

The emphasis on Ava's new title wasn't lost on her, neither was the tone of utter condemnation.

I'll get the same reaction from Ryan, thought Ava and the certainty twisted her heart. She cared nothing for the opinion of this civil servant, or of anyone else, but she could not have Ryan thinking badly of her, no matter what the cost.

"I'll make a start today," said Ava abruptly and she pressed the red button to end the call.

Leaning her head back on the sofa, she bit her lip, then stopped, thinking of Ryan's words whenever she did that. Her day was ruined; her week was ruined. Instead of making the house nice with all their new things, she'd have to go to Primrose Cottage and begin to sort out the decades of stuff her mother had left there.

Primrose Cottage. What a stupid name to give to such a dilapidated, run down and dismal place. Of course, it hadn't always been like that; it must have been new and shiny at one time, but Ava couldn't remember it. And she had no idea how long the house had stood there, how many years it had been built and how many of those years it had been owned and occupied by her parents.

She had another look on the internet for house clearance companies. Perhaps that would be the best idea; get rid of it without ever having to go near the place again. If she were still a single woman, with no ties and no other person in her life to have an opinion on it, she would do just that.

But there was Ryan.

***

The gates still hung open when Ava pulled up outside. She'd forgotten about getting them fixed, or getting a padlock. She'd had a glimmer of a thought about a bicycle lock, one of those with a plastic covered chain that she could loop around the gates and lock with a code.

But the idea had vanished from her mind the minute she'd got back in the car, when that awful neighbour had stopped her with questions she couldn't answer. Or had no wish to answer.

Now she walked toward the house, pointing the remote back at the car as she went and clicking it. Even in this neighbourhood, she wouldn't leave her car unlocked. She squeezed through the opening between the huge, rusting iron and stopped in the driveway, staring up at the dirty and cracked windows, the peeling paintwork.

It was as though there were a shield, a forcefield like on Star Trek that was keeping her from taking even one small step forward. She tried, she tried really hard to force herself to move, to walk to the house, to push the key in the lock and open the door. And as she stood there, trembling, her heart began to beat faster and harder and she knew a sudden and irrational fear that she had to leave, now, before the house itself reached out and grabbed her, dragged her inside against her will. And nobody would hear her screams.

Just as that thought occurred to her, there was a movement at the side of the house, on the path that led around and into the back garden. Ava's heart leapt and she took an involuntary step backward. Someone was coming, a shadow was looming to drag her inside. She swallowed, talked herself out of the illogical notion and looked toward the sound.

It was that bloody neighbour, that woman she had met the other day. What was her name? Cheryl, that was it. Her blonde hair was still perfectly coiffed, making Ava wonder if the woman had a permanent hairdresser living in or at least visiting every morning. Or perhaps it was a wig. She must have had a make up artist as well, judging by the exquisite paintwork on her eyes and lips, her smooth cheeks.

"What are you doing?" Ava forced her voice to utter.

Cheryl stopped in her tracks.

"Oh," she said. "I'm sorry. I didn't know you were here. I thought I saw someone in the house, so I came to have a look."

Codswallop! Utter bullshit!

"Well, is anybody there?" Ava said.

"No, it seems not."

And never was.

"Still, better to be safe than sorry," said Cheryl. "How is Mrs Fisher?"

"I've no idea," Ava replied.

"Oh, I thought you would have visited her by now. It has been a few weeks."

Ava wasn't one for explaining herself, particularly not to someone she didn't know, someone who had no business being involved. This was no exception. She could tell her how she had been away on her honeymoon, repairing the damage her mother had caused, simply by existing, simply by choosing this time to leave the house she hadn't left in years.

How do I know that? thought Ava. She didn't, did she? She just assumed. The state of the house assured her that its occupants would be even filthier and more dilapidated. Still, that didn't mean she never went out, but Mrs Nosy Cheryl had said Shirley was a recluse. Perhaps that's where the idea came from.

Cheryl was still there, waiting for some sort of conversation on the subject. *Well, why not?*

"Tell me, Mrs Bradley," she said, "did my mother ever leave the house? Did she go out?"

A sort of animation fell over Cheryl's face at the prospect of answering the question and by so doing, perhaps learning more about the mysterious woman and her equally mysterious dwelling.

"Never," she said at once. "That's why I was so surprised when the police came to ask about her."

"The police came to you?"

"Well, not to me specifically. They were knocking at every door in the Lane, asking if anyone knew Mrs Fisher and if we knew about her next of kin."

Ava nodded thoughtfully, forced a small smile and turned back to the house. The forcefield had gone, thank God, but not the neighbour.

"You're going to make a start, then?" Cheryl called after her. "Do you want some help?"

Ava didn't turn round to face her, just closed her eyes and drew a deep breath to control her rising temper. She didn't have much of a temper, but since the day her mother had been found wandering the motorway, it had been growing like some untamed wild animal over which she had little control.

"Thank you, no," Ava replied at last, still not turning to look at her pursuer.

"Are you sure? I don't have anything else to do today."

I'll just bet you don't.

"No. I'll manage."

"Well, you know where I am if you change your mind," said the persistent neighbour. "Just across the road."

Ava kept walking, her steps slowing as she neared the front door, where she stopped and glanced behind to be sure Cheryl had returned to her own domain, where she would no doubt be on the telephone, telling all the other neighbours that Mrs Fisher's daughter was there, at Primrose Cottage, and she hadn't even been to see her mother.

"*Now what do you think of that?*" Ava could almost hear her saying.

She grinned, opened the door and had stepped inside the hall before the stink forced her back, like a physical push on her chest. She opened the door wider to let in some air. There was a smell, no a stench, a stench of rotting something and it was strong enough to fell an elephant. That was one of Gran's sayings, 'strong enough to fell an elephant', but it was so apt here and now she had to smile as she remembered Gran saying that about the smell of her husband's socks.

But this didn't have the rotten egg stench of unwashed socks. This was the sort of smell that wafted out of the fridge when something had gone rotten in there, but worse.

A terrible idea made Ava close her eyes and say a quick prayer. She hadn't asked the social worker if her mother had any pets; she hadn't even thought about it, just assumed that if there were any, someone would have done something about them.

But who? No one went inside the house, not once they'd tracked Ava down and they seem to have done that straight away, as soon as she was found. Surely that nosy neighbour would have peered through the windows, wouldn't she?

A sudden and intense urgency overwhelmed Ava and she hurried forward, into the kitchen where she was relieved to see the absence of animal feed bowls. Most people fed their pets in the kitchen, didn't they? Unless they had a utility room or something like that.

She opened the cupboards, all of them, each one forcing her to yank it open as though it were painted shut and once they were opened, the hinges collapsed and left the doors hanging.

There was no sign of any pet food, no dog or cat biscuits, no hamster or rabbit meal. Thank God!

These cupboards were from the late sixties, when kitchen cupboards were made of basic wood and painted in bright colours. These had once been dark green, a colour Ava loathed and would never have in her house, but they were so dirty it was difficult to say how long ago they'd been painted.

The back door didn't lead outside. Ava still clutched the keys in her hand and now she found one that looked like it would fit this door. She opened it, still afraid she might find some sign of a pet somewhere.

It was a utility room of sorts, fitted out inside an old fashioned lean-to, the precursor of today's conservatory. She took one step through the doorway and her shoe stuck to the surface of the floor. She looked down, saw the yellow grease, the brown stains that were unidentifiable, then she took a quick glance round to be sure there were no feed bowls here either. There was no smell of animal waste, which there certainly would be if a dog or cat had been shut in.

Ava breathed a sigh of relief. If an animal had starved to death while she was enjoying herself in Florida, she would never forgive herself.

She made her way back into the hall and stood for a moment, suddenly realising that she had known where the kitchen was to be found and now she knew without a doubt that the door to the right would lead her into the living room. And she knew what that room would look like, she knew about the stone fireplace that stretched along an entire wall, she knew about the sliding patio doors with aluminium frames. She knew the carpet would be a dirty dark blue with huge red roses woven into it.

It might have been updated, brought into the twenty first century, but judging by the kitchen and utility lean-to, it was doubtful.

Memories of this house were gradually seeping into her brain and all she wanted to do was turn and run away.

She was getting used to the smell now. It

smelled less like rotting meat and more like rotting food. Her mother had left this house some three weeks ago, and nobody had been in to empty the fridge.

Her perusal of the kitchen cupboards had been frantic, looking for evidence of a pet, but now she recalled that there was very little in those cupboards. That was why it was so easy for her to see no pet food, because of the sparse contents.

She went back into the kitchen. The fridge was a huge, cream coloured thing of the sort used in the fifties. Ava decided she didn't have quite enough courage to open it, not now. The stench didn't get any stronger as she approached the beast, so perhaps it wasn't coming from there.

She looked about for the light switch, just to see if the electricity was still running. There it was, almost black from decades of dirty fingers lighting up the dismal house. Ava pointed her finger and pushed the switch with the end of her fingernail; the overhead lightbulb gave a feeble glow and she glanced up to see it had no shade, just the naked bulb, a bulb so thick with filth it gave out only the mere temptation of light.

Ava then felt her stomach heave. Beside the bulb, attached to the ceiling with a drawing pin, was one of those old fashioned fly papers, the sort that were no longer for sale because of the easy access to arsenic they provided, and stuck to it were hundreds of dead, black flies.

Heading for the front door, Ava picked up speed as she went. Outside, she stood in the driveway and gulped in glorious fresh air, but even here, out in the open, she imagined she could still smell the awful stench of the inside of the house.

She ran to the gate and her car, clicking the remote to open it as she went, and jumped in, starting the engine before she had her seat belt on. She'd put that on when she got out of this road, turned the corner. If that damned neighbour came out now, she might be tempted to run her over.

CHAPTER SEVEN

Ava sat on the sofa, her feet curled up under her and drank hot chocolate. She loved hot chocolate, but had abstained while planning for the wedding. She wanted to lose a few pounds to look her best in the dress and she had no intention of ever putting those pounds back on. But she felt the need to indulge, felt entitled to indulge after the trip to Primrose Cottage.

But I only went in the kitchen.

Yes, she had only gone in the kitchen and that awful lean-to thing, and she hadn't gone anywhere else; now she wondered why that was. The place had terrified her and she had no idea why, only that she felt in danger every minute she spent there. She tried to tell herself she was only afraid of catching something deadly from the filth inside the house, but she knew that wasn't it. What she didn't know was what it actually was and not knowing frightened her even more.

Here in her own living room in her own house, she felt safe, safe and warm and loved. Ryan loved her, his mother and father loved her, and she was convinced that nobody who had lived in Primrose Cottage had ever loved her.

Gran had taken her away. Ava had known that for most of her life, but knowing wasn't the same as really remembering, not the same as feeling it. She had never known why Gran took her to live with her and she had never asked, not really. At least, she had once and Gran had said her mother couldn't cope. But Ava hadn't persisted, hadn't asked again.

Not for the first time, Ava wished with all her heart that Gran was still here to explain all this to her. Perhaps she should try a medium, see if she could contact Gran and discover the truth. But she always attended the medium evenings at the Spiritualist Church and Gran had never come through.

She reached for her laptop and began searching, once again, for house clearance people. She found three nearby who all had five and four star reviews, but none of them were available to speak to her. She left messages on their answering machines, knowing they wouldn't ring back until this evening, when Ryan would be home. He would never understand; he had already proven that.

She knew he would ask if she'd been to Primrose Cottage, if she'd found anything interesting. She couldn't tell him why she'd only gone into the kitchen, the lean-to, then fled in terror.

***

"If you really can't face it," said Ryan, pushing his empty dinner plate aside, "I'll go. I'll clear the place out."

She was already shaking her head.

"No."

"You can't just let it all be thrown away," he persisted. "There might be valuable stuff there, you never know." He reached across the table and covered her hand with his own. "We should do it together," he said. "That's obvious. Leave it till Saturday, then we can spend the whole weekend there."

"What? Sleep there, you mean?"

The idea horrified Ava and she couldn't believe he was suggesting it.

"Well, no, it's not far away. We can come back here to sleep, unless you want to stay there."

"Certainly not. You have no idea how filthy the place is; it's absolutely disgusting."

"Then we'll leave early, make a start, go out for lunch then carry on till the evening. It'll all be easier with a schedule."

It's only Monday, she thought. *I've got the rest of the week to do it before the weekend, before Ryan sets foot in that house and discovers...what?*

Her heart sank, tears bunched in her throat. She wished to God she knew what she was so afraid of.

***

Ava decided to visit Ryan's mum and dad the following morning. She was biding her time, wasting it more like, trying to put off the inevitable visit to Primrose Cottage.

She hadn't seen much of Liz and Joe since she had returned from the honeymoon and she missed them. It was a surprise visit; she hadn't rung first to make sure they'd be home but it would be okay for her to call. She knew it would. They hardly ever went out, never went shopping together or on holiday and Ava knew it was an unspoken need to always be there, just in case. There was always the chance that Melanie might come home and it was sod's law that she would come when they were both missing. Wouldn't it be the ultimate horror if she did and there was no one home to meet her?

"Ava, darling!" Liz cried as she pulled her into her arms on the doorstep. "How wonderful of you to think of us."

"Of course I think of you, Liz. You know that. I've got a few more days before I have to go back to work."

She couldn't help but look at the new portrait on the wall, a pastel painting of the altered photograph of the wedding group, the bride and groom and the bridesmaids. Only this one showed an extra bridesmaid, this one included Melanie, dressed in the same pink lace dress as the others. The friend who had manipulated the picture had aged Melanie's image to be around the age she would have been now. Or would be now, depending on how much hope still lingered.

"It's clever, isn't it?" said Liz. "I'm so thankful to you both for having it done for us."

"It's the least we could do."

"She would have looked lovely, wouldn't she?" Liz was silent for a little while longer, staring at the picture, then her voice broke as she went on: "do you think one day she might see it herself?"

Ava was at a loss for words. She firmly believed that Melanie was dead and deep down, she was sure Liz knew it too. Ryan rarely mentioned his sister, so she had no idea what sort of hope he clung to. In fact, the only time he'd really let slip how much he cared was when he asked Ava to have Melanie's favourite colour for the bridesmaids' dresses.

She put her arm around her mother-in-law and gave her a hug and a kiss on the cheek, but she made no reply. She wanted to assure her that Melanie could see it, that she was in spirit and might even be there with them today. But she couldn't say it, not when Liz still clung to the hope that her daughter might still be alive somewhere.

"I'm lucky really," said Liz quietly. "I've got a good husband, a wonderful son and he has a wife who is so good to me, so loving. And I love you, Ava, I do, but…"

"But?"

"But wouldn't it make everything just perfect if Melanie were to come home now?"

She caught back a sob, turned away to wipe her eyes, then moved toward the sofa. Ava had no idea how to answer her, so she only followed to sit beside her and give her a hug.

"Joe's making tea," Liz said as she settled down. "Tell me all about your mother and how she is getting on in the nursing home. Is her condition permanent or just something they can control with drugs? I know someone who they thought had Alzheimer's and it turned out to be really high blood pressure that was making her confused."

Ava didn't want to answer, only wanted to let her ramble on and hope she didn't pause for a reply. Liz did that sometimes and it made things difficult when one wanted to get in a word, but on this occasion, Ava would have welcomed it. She wasn't so fortunate; Liz stopped talking and looked at her expectantly.

"I haven't seen her since we came home," she said.

"Oh, well, I suppose you know best."

"I see no point," said Ava. "After all, she hasn't a clue who I am."

"But you should still visit, just in case she suddenly remembers, don't you think?" Before Ava had time to think of an answer, Liz spoke again. "Sorry, dear. It's up to you, of course."

Perhaps Liz would be the one person who might understand how she felt. She was a very compassionate woman and her own personal tragedy might help her to empathise.

"You must understand," said Ava. "I don't know her. I haven't seen her since I was six years old. I've had nothing to do with her and I feel nothing for her. How should I?"

"But she's your mother," said Liz.

Those were the words she expected to hear from everybody, so why should she think Liz would be any different?

"No, she isn't," Ava insisted. "She gave birth to me, but she is not my mother. I have no mother. You are the closest thing I have to a mother since Gran died."

Liz reached across the short expanse between them on the sofa and covered her hand with her own.

"Would you like me to come with you?" she

said.

No! I don't want you to come with me! I want you to understand why I don't ever want to see her!

"I'll think about it," was all she said.

Ryan had to work late that night and Ava felt a little guilty at being glad of it. There was nothing on television to hold her interest, her mind was too busy with the indecision that now occupied it.

She took her book and went to bed early, when it was only just getting dark, and fell asleep straight away. She had been looking forward to reading the next chapter, but the words couldn't obscure the thoughts that chased each other around her head.

She felt too small for the enormous bed. It was a four poster, double, big enough for two adults, and Ava's mother had moved her there that day. She said her own room was too small, that she was a big girl now and needed a bigger bed in a bigger room. It was a monster of a bed and she couldn't understand why she should need such a huge bed. That night she found out.

It was her sixth birthday when he came in, telling her he had a special treat for her, that now she was all grown up she was old enough to be his special girl.

She relived every second of what happened next and she remembered hearing the television from downstairs. Her mother was still awake; Ava knew that if she screamed she would hear her. So she did, she screamed as loud as she could while the weight of her father almost crushed her, and he made no attempt to silence her, just let her scream.

But nothing happened. Her mother didn't come to rescue her; perhaps the television was too loud, perhaps she didn't hear her.

"I'll tell Mummy," she told him.

He laughed. She didn't understand why until she had cried herself to sleep, till she had seen the red stain on her bed sheet in the morning, till she went to tell her mother what had happened.

Shirley only glanced at her, pursed her lips and shook her head.

"You're a big girl now," she said. "You should know about these things. All he's doing is helping you to learn them."

The sound of Ryan's key in the front door woke her, or it may have been the sense of betrayal that had shattered her trust. She didn't know for sure, but the next thing she knew, Ryan was taking off his jacket and hanging it in the wardrobe.

"Still awake?" he said. He leaned over and kissed her, then wiped her cheeks with his thumbs. "You've been crying. What's wrong?"

"Bad dream," she said.

He finished undressing and slipped into the bed beside her, gathered her into his arms.

"What was it about? Do you remember?"

"I think it was a memory," she said. "I think I

know why I'm afraid to go into that house."

And now I know why I always hated the word 'mummy'.

And she did. Whenever she heard a child call its mother by that name, Ava had always shuddered and decided that no child of hers would ever use the word.

"Afraid? I didn't know you were afraid to go there." Ryan pulled her closer to him and kissed her cheek, brushed her hair away from her wet face. "I'm so sorry. I thought you just didn't want to for some reason. I didn't understand."

"Neither did I," she said quietly. "It was this dream; I suppose it was on my mind, the house, I mean. It was as though I was there again, a little girl, and I felt so helpless."

"Why?"

"I think I was molested, by my father. That's why Gran took me to live with her."

She felt his chest move as he drew a sharp breath, felt the ensuing sigh that escaped him.

"Oh, darling," he said. "If that's true, I can't blame you for not wanting to go there."

"I think that now I remember that, I'll be able to face it."

He shook his head.

"No. I don't want you to go there without me."

"I can do it now, I know I can."

"Well, if you're sure. I still think there might

be some valuable stuff there and if there is, you deserve it. Perhaps we can visit your mother, see if she can remember anything. They say that people with dementia can remember what happened years ago, but not what happened yesterday."

"No," Ava said. "I don't want to see her."

"Why not? Surely she would have protected you if she had known."

Ava allowed her lips to rest on his nipple, making him stir and cursing it because this was definitely not the time.

"She did know," said Ava. "I'm sure she knew what he was doing and she did nothing to stop him. She even condoned it. I remember everything."

And she did. She recalled the day her grandmother had called to see them. It was just after her birthday and she hadn't seen her to give her the present she'd bought. She was Ava's mother's mother and usually she would take Ava to see Gran on her birthday, but this year she hadn't. This year Ava had spent hours in that deep bath, the smell of sandalwood invading her senses.

Her heart jumped; she had always hated the smell of sandalwood. Now she knew why. Her mother had done that, had washed her in the 'grown-up' bath, the big, Victorian monstrosity that had always been forbidden to Ava before that day.

Then she'd had the 'special' present from her father and it was a week later when Gran turned up. A week or thereabouts; Ava couldn't remember exactly. It seemed the special present wasn't to be confined to her birthday.

All Ava knew was that week seemed to go on forever and she had no one to turn to. She couldn't get to Gran's house on her own and how was she to know that she wouldn't say the same thing, that she was a big girl now?

But Gran was angry. She'd pressed the buzzer on the electric gates but nothing had happened, no one had pressed the control inside the house to open them.

"She'll clear off if we ignore her," said Ava's father.

"I'll have to let her in." That was her mother and as she got to her feet, he yelled, making Ava jump.

"I said leave it!" he shouted.

Ava was in the garden, the windows were open and she heard every word. She went round the side of the house to the front driveway and saw through the wrought iron gates that it was Gran.

Her heart jumped with joy. She loved her Gran and she knew she'd have a present for her birthday, a present she would enjoy. So she ran to the gates and pressed the button there that would open them.

She fell into Gran's arms, she was so pleased. Then she was suddenly sure that if she told Gran, she wouldn't tell her it was all fine and she was a big girl. There was something about the way Gran talked to her, cuddled her, that was different to the way her mother always behaved with her. She hardly ever cuddled her, hardly ever even spared her a kind word.

Gran would understand if she told her. So she did. She whispered in her ear about her father's nightly visits to her bedroom, about her mother's assurance that he was teaching her how things were in the big wide world.

Gran hugged her closer and Ava could feel her trembling, then she turned back to her car. Ava thought she was going away, but she turned back and took her hand, led her to her car and lifted her inside. Gran got into the driver's seat and drove away and that was the last time she saw her parents or their house.

"I'm sorry, love," Gran said. "You'll have to leave your toys; we'll get some new ones."

"And my clothes?"

"Yes, but they are easy to replace."

Ava just nodded. She didn't know if they'd be able to get a dress the same as her favourite one, but that didn't really matter. She had one special toy, a stuffed Bugs Bunny who went everywhere with her, and leaving him was very hard, but she knew she'd be okay now.

After Gran had made her toast and marmite and sat her in front of the television, she went into the other room to make a phone call.

"She's staying with me," Gran said, trying to keep her voice low. "If you even attempt to get her back, I'll report the whole thing to the police and he'll be put away where he belongs. I should have guessed he'd do something like this."

Ava knew she was not intended to hear, but she did and she felt secure again, except for one thing. Who would look after Bugsie?

***

"Are you sure you don't want to wait till the weekend?" Ryan was saying as he slipped into his jacket and picked up his briefcase. "We can go together. It will be easier for you."

"No. I'll be fine now I know the truth." She reached up to kiss him goodbye. "I'll see you tonight."

As she watched him go, a memory reared up to steal away the pleasure of that kiss. It wasn't a clear memory, not vivid enough to pin down, but it was there all the same, like a long and dark shadow blocking out the sunlight. There had been a lot of those shadows reaching for her since Shirley Fisher was found wandering on the motorway. Now she hoped that knowing the truth would chase them all away.

She shook off the feeling and went upstairs to shower and dress. She would start on this bloody house today, she was determined, then get someone to clear out the rest. She'd have to get cleaners in as well, possibly decorators.

The house was a mess, as though the woman who had lived there was a hoarder, and perhaps she was. How would Ava know, after all?

Dressed in jeans and checked cotton blouse and feeling fresh and clean, she arrived at the still broken gates of Primrose Cottage. She had stopped at a bicycle shop on the way there and purchased a padlock and chain, just to keep out nosy Cheryl and anyone else who thought they had a right to peer through the windows.

Ava had nothing with her but a can of fresh air spray and a roll of plastic dustbin bags, ready to throw away almost everything. She planned to spend at least the entire morning there, then she'd go home and take another shower. After her last visit, she was sure she would need it.

The door still creaked when she pushed it open. It seemed that her mother hadn't left the place in years, so how she got her shopping was a mystery. Perhaps there was a computer somewhere or perhaps she had a smartphone and did all her shopping online. Judging by the confused state of her when Ava and Ryan went to the nursing home, it seemed unlikely.

That smell hit her again but this time she was ready for it and pointed her can of spray into the air. Then she started opening windows, at least the ones that could be opened. Most were sealed shut by long forgotten grease and grime and Ava was scared to push too hard, in case she went right through the glass. It seemed to be very thin, the glass, not like the double glazed units she had in her own house, or that Ryan's parents had in theirs. She recalled vaguely viewing a house when they were looking that needed modernising and one of the things the agent said was that the glass was not up to modern safety standards. That meant, she supposed, that a child could easily have an accident and go right through it.

That's what this glass was like, brittle and thin. It was also opaque with dirt and dust, not to mention more grease. She wondered if the woman ever did any housework; apparently not.

She opened the back door from the lean-to into the large, overgrown garden and stood staring at the expanse for a long time. There was the swing right at the bottom, rusted now, its chains creaking as they moved in the wind.

Ava remembered playing on that swing. She recalled it as vividly as though it were yesterday, sitting and swinging high with a man pushing her. It was him, her father, the man she trusted to push her higher and higher while she laughed till her ribs hurt.

But that was before, before she became a big girl. Feeling her lip begin to tremble, Ava bit down on the soft flesh to keep it still and turned back to the inside of the house. She went through to what had been the lounge, where the smell was fainter, where it hung in the air like the memories the whole place conjured up.

How could anyone relax in this room? The dust was so thick it stank and Ava covered her nose and mouth with her hand. She was sure the grime would find its way into her mouth, down her throat, enter her stomach and all her organs and begin to rot them from the inside.

She shuddered and shook herself out of the illogical idea. Death by dust; there was a new one.

The sofa and armchairs were of the style popular in the forties, deep and soft with high, curved arms and that velvety embossed covering. There was no telling what colour they had once been; they were filthy. Ava hit the sofa arm and a grey cloud of dust flew up and assaulted her. She jumped back, wishing she'd brought a scarf or something, one of those masks they used in hospitals. They were available at chemists, she was sure, so she would stop and get some on her way home.

She turned back toward the door and crossed the wide hall to another door, expecting it to be at the front of the house. But it wasn't; it was at the back and the only window was a frosted glass one high up near the ceiling.

For some reason she saw that window first, before she'd even looked at the room itself. A memory slapped her in the face as soon as she opened the door, before she looked round at the ancient, Victorian sunken bath, the gold taps, the pull chain on the cistern.

Her heart began to beat faster. There it was, the huge sunken bath she had hoped she only dreamed about. It wasn't as big as she remembered, but then she had been so small then. Now she couldn't swim in it, but the memory of it still lingered and there, on the shelf above it, was the bath oil with the faded label – sandalwood.

Ava spun around and slammed the door behind her, hurried back to the living room and the relatively normal atmosphere, if one could ever call a room with so much dirt 'normal'.

There were no memories associated with this room, nothing here to terrify her.

Glancing around the room, she caught sight of the old fashioned fireplace, still containing some cold ash. A memory leapt up at her now, a memory of that fire, blazing with hot coals and flames escaping up the chimney. She remembered the snow clinging to the windows outside, remembered loving that warm fire in the winter, remembered sitting in front of it until her legs were scorched and a mottled pattern spread over them. She recalled how she never wanted to leave it to go to bed, her own, small bed. She was surprised, shocked even to realise there was a good, comforting memory in be found in this house.

There was an old, brown suitcase tucked between the sofa and the sideboard. It was quite small, one of those sort of cardboard ones they used to use in the fifties and earlier. It was cracked across the top and as Ava pulled it out, the handle came off in her hand.

Picking it up in her arms, she felt its weight and wondered what on earth could be inside. Was Shirley planning on going somewhere? Perhaps she had packed her things and set off without the case, found her way to the motorway and ended up in the care of Social Services.

She couldn't sit on this furniture, that was certain, so she carried the case outside, thankful that she had left the back door open, and hauled it onto the wrought iron garden table she'd seen just outside the door. Then she went back inside to find a tea towel, a cloth to wipe the damp and grimy seat of the matching chair before she sat on it.

The sun was shining through the clouds now, warming her face and she closed her eyes for a moment and recalled the laughter on that swing. She shook herself out of the memory. She couldn't sit here and do this, start to believe she'd had an idyllic, happy childhood. She knew that was a lie, she knew that happy family scene hadn't lasted.

That was when the music started. It was very faint, so faint that she couldn't even guess the tune or what sort of music it was, but it was coming from the other side of the trees. Ava thought it must be a neighbour, playing a radio, but she didn't think there were any close enough to hear.

Shrugging, she dismissed the idea and turned to the suitcase. She would see what this suitcase held, then look about the rest of the house. If she found nothing of any value, the house clearance people would be the next step. If Ryan didn't understand, that was his problem.

Already this house and its owner have caused a rift between us. No more!

The catches snapped open and Ava threw back the lid. Once again, dust assaulted her, making her lean back and away. But Ava was surprised; the case wasn't full of clothes, as she expected. It was full of photographs, old black and white photographs mostly, but there were also faded colour ones. These pictures had been taken many, many years ago and the colour ones were polaroid.

And they were all of little girls.

CHAPTER EIGHT

They were only headshots, some full length poses but nothing nasty. Ava held her breath as she rummaged through the hundreds of cracked and faded ancient pictures.

There was no one there that she recognised and she thought it likely these pictures were taken when her mother was just a child herself. But not her father; he was many years older than his wife, possibly twenty or even thirty years. Perhaps more.

She should know, but she didn't. What she really wanted to do was to take the whole lot to the incinerator and put a match to them. She was making up her mind about that when one face among the others caught her attention.

She knew that face. The picture was black and white, the surface peeling somewhat, but even so she recognised that face. She had seen it before, in an old photograph album belonging to her Gran. That photograph was of her grandparents on the beach with their own little girl, Shirley, Ava's mother.

That's who this was, Ava's mother. The girl in the picture was about nine or ten years old, perhaps a little older but not much. She was wearing one of those old swimsuits, the sort that was made of cotton with an elasticated body. Smiling, she was, laughing at the camera, as though someone were there, someone important to her.

Ava's imagination conjured up a moving film and it would have this child pushing back her hair, laughing, and the man with the camera would be talking to her, making her laugh.

But there was no moving film, just the emptiness, the silence, the dust of this filthy house. There was a noise, though, very faint. That radio again, that distant sound from one of the neighbours.

Ava shut the lid on the suitcase but she couldn't seem to get the catches to work so she carried it under her arm until she got inside. She shoved it onto the sofa, left the few that had fallen on the floor and, grabbing her handbag, she took out the keys and headed to the front door.

She needed to think, needed to be in her own, clean house, sit on her own clean sofa and wonder why anyone had a suitcase full of old snapshots of little girls.

***

Ava thought she had been inside Primrose Cottage for an hour at the most. All she had done was to open a few windows and doors and that bloody suitcase. But when she started her car and looked at the clock on the dashboard, she found she had been there for three hours.

What the hell had she been doing for three hours? She put her foot down and drove as fast as was safe out of Dog Kennel Lane. A swift glance to the side showed her Mrs Cheryl Nosy-Parker, conveniently pulling weeds in her front garden.

Ava smiled. Cheryl was dressed in designer trousers with a cashmere sweater and pearls, which Ava assumed were real. She would bet a week's wages this woman had never pulled weeds before in her entire life.

Perhaps she should ask her to help next time. It would be amusing to find out what Cheryl would think of the grime and the dust and the photographs. Especially the photographs.

At home she made tea and switched on the television, turned off the sound. She just wanted the illusion of not being alone while she sipped from her mug and closed her eyes to think about those pictures.

There were at least a hundred of them; the case would barely close, and so old. Ava's father was born during the second world war, perhaps even just before it even started in the thirties. He could have taken them himself, but why?

You know why, don't you? That little inner voice was nagging her again. It was her conscience talking, she was sure of it, someone to argue with who would argue back but didn't have any real say in matters.

But the voice was right this time. She did know, because she now knew the reason her gran had taken her to live with her when she was just six years old. And she remembered something else Gran had told her; she remembered that her mother had been only sixteen when she married her father.

Gran's voice cut through her thoughts, a faint whisper right at the back of her mind, begging to be heard. Ava's father was a friend, a best friend of her grandfather. He went everywhere with them; he could drive, had a car and not everyone did in those days. He it was who took them on outings to the seaside, he it was who spent Christmas with them as he had no one else and they enjoyed his company.

But his company was given less and less to Ava's grandfather and more and more to Shirley herself. He would take her along the beach, looking for crabs and collecting shells. There was nothing suspicious about such closeness, not in those days.

Ava's grandparents came from a more innocent age, when anything not quite nice was covered up for fear of scandal. They would never have suspected their best friend, who did so much for them, of having anything but honourable intentions toward the whole family.

But now Ava could see what was happening then; he had been grooming Shirley, making her love him so that she would keep his secrets and do anything for him.

And as soon as she was old enough, he married her.

Gran and Grandad had been dead set against it. They had even locked her in her bedroom to try to stop it, but she escaped and they drove to Gretna Green to be married.

Ava had always thought that romantic; now she was not so sure. Shirley was little more than a child then and he was almost an old man.

Now she had found, among her father's things, a photograph of her mother when she was a child, a real child about nine years old with an awkward smile and a ribbon in her hair.

And all those other little girls whose photographs filled that suitcase? Who were they?

***

"How did you get on at the house?" Ryan asked after he had greeted her with a kiss on his arrival. "Anything valuable there?"

"Not that I saw," she replied.

I really don't want to talk about it. But he did, that was obvious. His eyes twinkled when he was excited about something and they twinkled now; he thought this house full of history was something to relish, not run away from.

"Well, perhaps there's more. It's an enormous house."

"How do you know?"

"I drove passed it, just to have a look," he answered. "You don't mind, do you?"

Yes! Yes I do mind! I don't want you contaminated by it!

She shook her head, pushed herself off the sofa and went into the kitchen to dish up the casserole that had been slow cooking all afternoon.

"No, I don't mind. I just don't like the place; I told you why."

He put his arms around her, held her close.

"I understand that, darling. Of course I do." He kissed her cheek, then released her to open the cutlery drawer and set the table for dinner. "As I said, it's up to you."

"I think I might get the house clearers in after all," she said.

"Really? Well, your choice, if you think that would be best."

No more was said about the house while they

ate and settled down to watch a film on television. But she couldn't concentrate; house clearers were no longer an option were they? Because who knew what else they might find in there? But would house clearers bother to look, or would they simply box it all up and dispose of it? She had no idea, but she was sure they'd be as keen to look for valuables as Ryan seemed to be.

She silently cursed her mother for giving her these problems, and just when she should be starting her life with the man she loved. Just when she should be happy.

"I think I'll have an early night," she said.

She leaned across and kissed Ryan, kissed him deeply and passionately. Before an old woman was found wandering on the motorway, a kiss like this would have fired her passions until she couldn't keep her hands off her husband. Now there was a little nagging doubt at the back of her mind, a little doubt which wondered if it was quite right to enjoy him so much. Sex should be about love, grown up love, not the abuse of a helpless child.

She climbed the stairs to her bedroom, saying a little quiet prayer that she could recapture that feeling, that need she had been enjoying until that bloody woman left her with a hell hole called Primrose Cottage.

It was not the same that night; Ava wondered if it would ever be the same again but she would never know if she didn't get on with clearing Primrose Cottage, distasteful task though it was, and putting it up for sale. What she really wanted to do was put a match to it.

***

She would be back at the office the following week. She had to finish at least going through everything, otherwise it would be weekends only and Ryan would insist on helping. Ava didn't want Primrose Cottage reaching out grabbing him, taking him away from her, turning him against her.

Was that illogical? Was it some sort of nightmarish fantasy? She didn't know, but she did know that she had to do this alone.

She left early, 7 am, before even Cheryl was awake and peering through her shutters. She got out of the car and pushed the broken gate just wide enough to drive through, then she made her way around the back of the house where no one would see her.

She hated nosy people, hated their poorly concealed curiosity and she wouldn't answer their questions, would never explain herself.

She had the back door keys as well as the

front and now she had let some fresh air into the lean-to and the kitchen, it was a better aroma that met her than the first time she was here.

There was that radio again, or maybe it was a television. Whatever it was, Ava couldn't understand where it could be coming from. She stood in the garden and looked about, searching for a neighbouring house that might be close enough for her to hear a sound from it. But there was nowhere, not that she could see anyway, and she settled for being thankful she didn't live close to someone who would play their music so loud.

It didn't matter; it wasn't important, not now. Now, she needed to clear out everything and she started with that dilapidated brown suitcase. She stuffed all the photographs back inside it and took it out to her car. She had no idea what she was going to do with it, but she couldn't leave it here.

In the corner of the living room stood a scroll top desk, which Ava thought might be worth something. It depended a lot on its age, whether it was a genuine antique or a reproduction, but she couldn't care about that right now.

She pushed at the lid, but it was firmly stuck. Ava reached into her handbag for the bunch of keys the social worker had given her and found one that looked as though it might fit the desk. It was stiff to turn, as though it hadn't been opened in a very long time, but eventually it moved and she was able to push up the scrolled top.

An overflow of paper assailed her. It had all been squashed in, the lid forced down to keep it back and now it covered the floor and the chair in front of it, some of the paper yellowed with age.

Ava gave a deep sigh of resignation. She would have to go through all of this stuff and that would take up even more time. She pushed back the chair and sat down, reached for a handful of papers and allowed her eyes to skim over them.

Bills. Invoices and receipts for invoices, some of them going back years, not something anyone would want to keep. Most people kept receipts for a few months, sometimes a few years, but twenty years? Thirty?

It was something of a relief to realise that this lot could go into the incinerator in the garden, yet as more receipts poured out of the desk, the heading for a photographic supply company caught her eye. It was dated some fifteen years ago and listed there were items for use in a dark room, a place where a photographer could develop and print his own pictures, without any chemist or photographic shop seeing them.

So what was he afraid of? What had he photographed that he didn't want seen by anyone else? Somewhere in this house there must be a dark room, a place with no windows where newly printed photographs might be pegged onto a line to dry.

It was probably in the cellar, or cellars since the place was so big. It was where wealthy people used to store their fine wines when this house was built, but who knew what was down there now?

Something else to fill her with dread.

It was a bright day, no wind, so it wouldn't take long and she knew what she was going to do with those papers. But she wouldn't burn the photographs, not until she had thought more about them. There was nothing nasty there, just innocent photographs, just like any other family photographs, so why did she feel so afraid of them?

Ava made up her mind then. That suitcase and its contents were going into the incinerator, along with this mountain of wood pulp in the desk.

Grabbing the roll of black plastic rubbish sacks, she tore one off and stuffed all the papers from the desk into it. She twirled it around to make a handle then picked it up and reached for the suitcase, forgetting that she had put it in her car.

She went outside and opened the boot, pulled out the case, stuffed it under her arm and carried it to the incinerator before going back inside the house.

In her bag were the matched she had remembered to bring and now she took the black sack into the garden to join the suitcase. She tipped the contents of the sack into the incinerator, struck a match and waited for the inflammable, dry paper to catch light. It was half burned away when she glanced at the suitcase and changed her mind again.

Not yet. Something was stopping her and deep down she knew what it was. It was not normal for anyone to have a suitcase full of photographs of children that were not theirs and if Ava were to burn them all without looking to be sure, she would never forgive herself.

She told herself that her father, a man who was obviously attracted to little girls, had taken photographs wherever he went, wherever he saw a pretty child. But most of these pictures were taken in an era when nobody recognised paedophiles, nobody spoke about abuse because of the scandal. What would the neighbours say? That was the be all and end all of life back in the forties and fifties, even later.

Ava had gone to school with a girl who she

later discovered had been fathered by her own grandfather, her and her three siblings. But nobody would admit it or have the disgusting old pervert put in prison. Think of the scandal!

Sometimes she believed those innocent times were worth preserving, but when she heard of people like that grandfather and her own father, she was glad of today when things were open, when nobody was ashamed of events that were no fault of their own.

Putting the lid back onto the incinerator, Ava heaved the suitcase under her arm again and took it back inside the house. She just couldn't bring herself to burn it and its contents; it would be like burning the memory of all these innocent little faces.

There seemed to be nothing else in the living room to explore so Ava took herself and her roll of rubbish bags into the dining room. This room was a different matter entirely. It was like one of those carefully laid dining tables that they had in stately homes, or would have been had it not been for the dust.

The plates and matching cups and saucers, the soup tureen, everything looked like really expensive bone china. Ava picked up one plate and turned it over to look at the stamp on the bottom which declared it to be of a very valuable make. Finally, the thing Ryan had been wanting to find, something of value. But did she really want to take it away and sell it separately? She wondered if she had the right to do that, or whether it should all go toward the nursing home fees.

Still, she deserved something for having to sort through the grime and the junk. She found some newspaper in a pile in the corner of the room and began to wrap the crockery carefully for transportation. But as she opened up the sheets of yellowing paper to pad it, she noticed the date on this one was 1956. Intrigued, she held it closer to her eyes and read, expecting to find some quaint news items from that era. Instead she saw a face that was vaguely familiar, one of the faces in one of the pictures in that suitcase.

The black and white picture was of that same little girl and it was accompanied by an editorial, detailing the disappearance of this child. Ava pulled out her phone and opened 'notes' to write the name. When she got home, she intended to look this up on the internet; there was bound to be something about it.

Yet if this child was one that went missing, what about all the others?

CHAPTER NINE

Ava couldn't wait to get out of the house, get home and have a hot shower. They were going out that evening, going to Ryan's parents for dinner as this was the anniversary of the day Melanie had gone missing.

The local newspaper would have an article about all the children that had disappeared at the same time and Ava wanted to see that. They always printed photos of the children and she wanted to see if any of them matched the pictures in that suitcase.

She had managed to find two strong cardboard boxes in which to pack the dinner service and now she struggled to get them into the house, where she left them on the kitchen table while she made her way to the bathroom and pulled off her clothes. She felt like burning them, too, but that would be ridiculous.

As she stood under the water and washed off the grime of Primrose Cottage, she realised that Melanie could be one of those pictures in that suitcase. She could be, except they were all very old pictures, even the few faded colour ones, all taken far too long ago to include one of her. Was it possible they were all Melanies? And was she attracted to Ryan because his sister fell prey to another like her father? Perhaps there was some higher power steering her toward him, for the purpose of making her understand better.

She dressed with care. Ryan was to meet her at his parents' house and the meal would be macaroni cheese, because that was Melanie's favourite. Ava had attended this anniversary dinner every year since she met Ryan and it got no easier as the years went by.

This year would be even harder for Ava. This year was when the doubts started to creep in. She and Ryan had always promised each other they would have no secrets, but now she couldn't make up her mind whether to tell him what she had discovered. But what had she discovered? A suitcase full of children's photographs and a desk full of receipts, evidence that her father had developed his own photographs?

But one of pictures, one of those children was a missing girl, just like his sister, and that's what made her wonder if she should tell. Or was this one secret she should keep to herself?

Ryan opened the door for her, greeted her with an affectionate kiss and hug. They both knew this would be a gruelling supper, one where they would have to be careful what they said, lest it upset Liz even more than usual.

The macaroni cheese was perfect, just as Liz

had cooked it on this day every year for the past seventeen years. Although she never said so, Ava thought that Ryan's mother hoped, deep down in her soul, that the meal would tempt her little daughter home. It was irrational and it was heartbreaking.

The two men cleared away and loaded the dishwasher, while Liz followed Ava into the living room with her coffee and sat down beside her. She looked expectant, as though she wanted to tell her daughter-in-law something, but it was something that was hard to say.

After a few minutes, Liz put her hand gently on Ava's arm and gave her a little smile.

"Can I ask you something, dear?"

"Of course," said Ava. "I can't promise to answer, though."

Liz smiled and nodded, removed her hand.

"I think I heard you say you belonged to the Spiritualists, that you visited mediums sometimes," she said.

Ava knew what was coming next and she wasn't sure what advice to give. She had a strong feeling that neither Ryan nor his father would approve of what Liz was proposing. Still, it wasn't up to them, was it?

"I have," she answered. "Especially when my Gran died."

"And did you find it useful? Do you think it

was genuine?"

"Yes, I did. But then I've always believed in spirits so perhaps my mind was a little too open." She grasped Liz's hand and squeezed it. "Why are you asking? You want to try to get in touch with Melanie?"

Liz nodded.

"Yes, I do. I've been thinking about it for a while now but it really is admitting that she has gone, isn't it?"

"That's true, but don't you already know that?"

Again, Liz nodded.

"I do, deep down. But I thought if I could get in touch with her, she might be able to tell me where..." she hesitated, caught back a sob, afraid to say the words.

"Where her remains are?" asked Ava.

"Yes. It would be so much easier if we had a grave to visit."

But do you really want to know what happened to her? Do you really want to know how she might have suffered?

Ava thought about little Leslie Ann Downey, that poor child who was tortured and murdered by the Moors Murderers back in the 1960s. The evil bastards recorded it all and her mother had to listen to it. Ava didn't believe that Liz would be able to cope with that, with hearing that desperate little voice for the rest of her life.

She also didn't understand the need to have a grave to visit, to give the child's remains a decent burial. Ava didn't believe in funerals; she was quite convinced that the corpse was merely an empty container, the soul contentedly going on in spirit and no longer suffering.

Surely Liz was better off not knowing, remaining in ignorance. But then, Ava wasn't a mother and had no idea that by not knowing, Liz could only imagine what her little girl had gone through and her imaginings were often worse than the truth.

"I'll take you," said Ava. "If that's really what you want. But it's never as clear cut as just asking and getting an answer. The mediums I see are genuine, but you need to be careful of charlatans. Unfortunately, there are a lot of them about."

And Ava was quite sure that if she didn't take Liz to one of the mediums she had seen, she would be prey to every charlatan out there.

"I'll make an appointment," she said.

"Make an appointment for what?" said Joe, Ryan's father who now entered the room with him.

Ava opened her mouth to answer, but Liz got there first.

"For her hairdresser," she said quickly. "I don't like this new one at my usual place."

Ava didn't contradict her, but she wasn't happy about arranging the visit without Ryan's father knowing. Still, it was none of her business. The couple didn't have that same honest relationship that Ava had with Ryan.

But even as she thought it, her heart sank. She hadn't told him about her mother, and she hadn't told him about the photographs she had found in the house. What's more, she wasn't sure that she ever would.

Damn that bloody woman! She felt like going straight to that fancy, overpriced nursing home and finding something heavy to hit her with. She had never felt real hatred for anyone in her entire life and the more she learned to despise her, the more memories that came bursting out of those locked doors in her mind.

***

Ava arranged the appointment with the medium, named Muriel, on a morning when Joe did some voluntary work at the local hospital, taking round the mobile library.

"Why haven't you told him?" she asked Liz when they pulled out of the driveway.

"He wouldn't understand," Liz replied. "He'd say I was wasting my money; he doesn't believe in this sort of thing."

"I'm surprised you do," said Ava.

"I'm not sure that I do really. But I'll try anything. You can't imagine what it's been like all these years, not knowing whether Melanie's alive or dead, not know what she went through. You know, you hear about kidnap victims kept prisoner for years."

That was true, of course, and Ava knew that, while she had thought Liz had accepted that Melanie was gone, she was still clinging to a vague hope that her daughter was still alive somewhere. Yet why would she want that? Because if Melanie was still alive, she'd be going through endless torture. Ava thought it would be better if she were dead, but then she had a firm belief in an afterlife and she wasn't a mother.

It wasn't a long journey, just into Cambridge. The medium was going to meet them at the Spiritualist Church as Ava thought it would seem more authentic to an unbeliever; or a half believer.

She pulled into the car park and switched off the engine, turned to her passenger.

"Okay?" she asked.

Liz nodded.

"I'm a bit nervous."

"No need. It's not like they have on the telly, you know. There won't be any knocking on tables and asking 'is there anybody there?' No 'Madam' anything and no gypsy type dressed up in fancy clothes. No crystal balls either, though there might be tarot cards."

"What does she do then?"

"She's just an ordinary woman with a gift. If there is anyone who wants to talk to you, they'll come through and she will hear them. If nobody does come through, it doesn't mean they're not there, just that they've moved on."

"So we're just supposed to believe what she says?"

"A certain amount of trust is necessary, yes, but you will know if she's telling you the truth. You will know if she has really reached a relative or friend."

Liz drew a deep breath.

"Okay, let's get it over with."

Liz opened the passenger door and swung her legs out of the car.

"It's not too late to change your mind, you know," said Ava.

"No. If I turn round now, I'll only keep thinking I should have gone through with it."

Ava pointed her remote fob at the car to lock it and led the way into the side door of the church. It was a large, brick building, a real church but without a graveyard round it, just a car park. Ava was still wondering if this was such a good idea.

The woman who greeted them with a handshake and a huge smile was about fifty, with a great surplus of weight and flesh. She wore a kaftan type dress which covered her enormous girth, but the bright yellow flowers on the fabric counter balanced any possible slimming effect of the loose garment.

"Come in, my dear," said Muriel. "Sit down and take my hand."

"Do you want me to stay, Liz?" said Ava. "It's up to you."

"Oh, yes, please. Do stay."

"There's no need to be scared," said Muriel. "The people who might come to speak through me are people who loved you before they passed over. Now they are in spirit, they still love you."

Liz swallowed hard and nodded while the huge hand covered hers and gave it a gentle squeeze. Muriel closed her eyes and smiled gently.

"I have a gentleman here," she said. Liz began to shake her head; she didn't want a gentleman. She wanted a little girl. "His name is Alf ... no Alan."

Liz's heart leapt. Her late father's name was Alan, but how could this woman have known that? She wondered then if Ava had booked this appointment in Liz's name and she had looked her up somewhere.

"How did you know?" she demanded.

"He's telling me, dear," said Muriel. "But there's no need to worry. Everyone is sceptical at first. You were close to him, weren't you? More than to your mother."

"My mother died when I was a child," said Liz, then wished she could take back the words. She shouldn't tell this woman too much, should she? Ava frowned at her. She had never been told about Liz's mother.

Muriel was nodding knowingly.

"Yes, he's telling me that," she said. She frowned, tilted her head to one side as though trying to listen more carefully. "Oh, dear. He wants me to tell you that it wasn't her fault, that you shouldn't blame her."

Liz's gasped and her eyes filled with tears, tears that started to spill over onto her cheeks. Ava took a clean tissue from her bag and passed it to her mother-in-law. If she'd known about this, she would never have brought her. She leaned across and touched her arm, but Liz only smiled.

"She died," said Liz. "Why should I blame her for that?"

"But you do, don't you, dear?" said Muriel. "She had no choice. He's telling me she had no choice."

Liz made no reply. This was all too much for her to take in and it wasn't her reason for coming to this woman.

"Enough of her!" she cried out, showing more animation and anger than Ava had ever seen in her before. "I want to know about my little girl."

Muriel looked at her curiously, then closed her eyes again. She was quiet for some minutes, frowning occasionally, then finally her eyes opened and compassion showed clearly in them.

"I'm so sorry, Elizabeth," she said. "I can find no sign of your daughter. It is possible she has crossed over already. I mean that she has moved on."

Liz was shaking, her tears soaking into the neck of her jumper. She jumped to her feet and ran from the room, while Ava pulled some money out of her purse to pay the medium.

"I'm sorry I couldn't help," said Muriel.

"When you say you could find no sign of her," said Ava, "what does that mean exactly? I mean what does it usually mean?"

"It could mean a lot of things, dear," said Muriel. "If you know she is in spirit, it could be that she is with those who love her and don't want her unsettled."

"Could it be that she isn't dead?" said Ava.

"Is there some doubt?"

"She was kidnapped, twelve years ago, when

she was just a child. If she's still alive, there's no telling what she is going through."

"Melanie," said Muriel. "He's telling me, Melanie."

"What else? What's he saying about Melanie?"

Muriel shook her head.

"Nothing else, just her name."

***

Ava caught up with Liz and found her leaning on the car. She had dried her tears, but looked angry now.

Ava pointed the remote fob at the car to unlock the doors and Liz rapidly jumped inside. It was as though she wanted to escape before anyone saw her, and perhaps she did.

Ava slipped behind the wheel and turned to her.

"Sorry," she said.

"For what? It wasn't your fault. I have to admit, I came here thinking it was all a scam and that the woman, Muriel, would say she had Melanie. She would have looked up old newspapers and perhaps seen a picture of me. I didn't expect her to get my father."

"It happens," said Ava. "What happened to your mother? Tell me to mind my own business if you like."

"She committed suicide," said Liz. "When I was twelve."

Ava felt the colour draining from her face. Here she had been wrapped up in herself and her own mother, she never considered that anything really bad had happened to anyone else. She cursed her own selfishness.

"I'm so sorry," she said, covering Liz's hand with her own. "All this business with my mother turning up, I never thought to even ask what sort of childhood you had."

"That's all right, dear," said Liz. "I do remember her, but I tend to think she must have been mentally ill to have done that. I try not to dwell. It's the same with your mother, though, isn't it? She is mentally ill, suffering from some sort of dementia."

"She might be mentally ill now," said Ava, "but she wasn't back then."

"You'd feel better if you try to forgive her."

Ava suppressed a cynical laugh.

"Never," she said.

"If she couldn't get Melanie," said Liz, "that must mean she's still alive, mustn't it?"

"Not necessarily. Spirits don't always come just because we want them to."

Having watched Liz disappear through her front door, Ava drove away towards her own home. It was getting late and she wanted her dinner; Ryan would be home soon and asking more questions about bloody Primrose Cottage.

But the traffic was bad due to an accident and he was already there when she opened the door and heard his voice, talking to someone on the telephone.

"That's her now, dad," he said. "I'll call you back."

She greeted him with a smile. The sight of him always made her heart skip, no matter how many times she saw him. He was so handsome, such kind blue eyes, darker blue than most and almost black hair. And such a sexy body. She walked quickly toward him and put her arms around him, kissed his lips, but there was a resistance there she had never felt before. It was only slight, barely perceptible, but it was there.

This would be something to do with that woman, the one who called herself her mother.

"What's wrong?" she asked.

"That was Dad on the phone," he replied. "He's annoyed that you took Mum to see a medium."

Ava moved away and looked up, her eyes meeting his. She frowned.

"She wanted to go," she replied. "She asked me to arrange it."

"But you shouldn't have taken her; you know

how distraught she is about Melanie."

Ava turned away from him and went into the kitchen, heard his footsteps following her. She put the kettle on, lifted the lid of the slow cooker to see how the dinner was doing, gave it a stir.

Her anger was rising.

"What was I supposed to tell her?" she demanded, turning back to face him. "You'd better ask your husband's permission?"

"No, but..."

"But what?"

"Don't you think you should have discussed it with me first?"

"Is this the start then?" she demanded, her voice rising along with her temper. "Now we're married, you think I need to ask your permission before I do anything?"

"That's not what I said. I said discuss it."

"Your mother has a brain," said Ava. "She shouldn't have to discuss anything with anyone. I took her to Muriel because she wanted to go and if I hadn't, she might have found a dishonest medium, a charlatan. Why should she have to ask anyone?"

"She doesn't but she's easily distressed."

"Everyone's easily distressed when it comes to your sister. They always will be."

The kettle began to boil, Ryan took two mugs off the mug tree and spooned coffee into them, then poured the boiling water over them. He knew he'd gone about this all wrong, that Ava wouldn't stand for being told what to do. And she was right; his mother should be allowed to make up her own mind about what she did.

"Well?" he said. "Did she get in touch with Melanie?"

"Get in touch? Are you being sarcastic?"

"No."

"And if I say 'yes' she did, you'll think it was all a scam."

"When have I ever given you the impression that I thought it was a scam?" he said. "I've always respected your beliefs."

"But you don't share them. You think Spiritualism is a parlour game. It isn't; it's a religion."

"I know that." He sipped his coffee. "I'd like to know what happened."

Picking up her mug, she returned to the living room and sank down onto the sofa. She was trying to calm herself, trying not to be angry. She knew that both he and his father were acting out of concern for Liz, but that didn't make it any easier to tolerate.

"Actually, it was your grandfather who came through," she said. "Your mother's father, Alan wasn't it?"

"Not Melanie?"

Ava shook her head.

"No. And now your mother is convinced she's still alive." She put the mug on the side table and let out a huge sigh. "So it seems the men in the family are right. I shouldn't have taken her. I thought it would put her mind at rest once and for all, to know that her child's spirit lives on and is happy. It's done more harm than good."

CHAPTER TEN

The sun knew it had no right to shine on Primrose Cottage. That's what Ava felt when she returned to the house and went into the garden. It was a warm day but still the sun struggled to break through the grime on the windows and she felt sure it was only that grime which was holding the glass in the dilapidated frames.

She had to get this done, starting with every cupboard and drawer in the house. She found more receipts and invoices, electricity bills, gas bills, even a bill for her father's funeral. Odd, she'd never really known when he died before. The invoice and receipt were dated July, twelve years ago, just a week after Melanie disappeared.

She vaguely recalled Gran talking to someone on the phone and telling them that he was dead, but she didn't take too much notice, didn't even think to ask about it. By that time, he was a stranger to her, someone she didn't even remember and didn't want to.

She tossed the receipt into the plastic sack, along with the other papers. The dead had no need of funerals. That was why she couldn't understand Liz's eagerness to find her little girl's remains and give them what she called a 'decent burial'. Still, she might not understand it, but she was determined to respect it.

It only took a couple of hours to get all the rubbish into dustbin liners, but that was when Ava realised she might just need to hire a skip. There would be far more bags of rubbish than she expected. Ryan's car was bigger; it was an estate. She could bring that at the weekend, or maybe swap vehicles with him.

She'd only given herself until the weekend to finish the job. Now she lifted the bags stuffed with out of date paperwork into the back garden. There was too much of it to burn and she saw no reason to shred it. It was too old to be used for identity theft, and it wasn't in her name anyway so she really didn't care. She'd take it all to the recycling centre on her way home.

Next were the rooms upstairs, up two short flights which creaked alarmingly, making Ava wonder if they were safe. After feeling that the first step was not quite solid, she felt for her mobile phone to be sure she had it to hand, in case she needed to call for help. Hanging on tight to the banister rail the rest of the way, her hand coming up thick with grey dirt, she made it safely to the landing.

The higher she climbed, the darker it got and on reaching the top, the first thing she did was to find the light switch. The lightbulb wasn't particularly bright; looking up, she saw that the shade was dark blue and the bulb had thick dust stuck to it. She shuddered, grimaced as the stench hit her.

It stank up here even worse than downstairs. It stank of stale sweat, urine, general staleness and just plain shit. It smelled as though someone had forgotten to clear up after their dog or cat, and although Ava had established that there were no pets, that didn't mean there had never been any.

She hurried to open every window she could find, in all five bedrooms. She stopped, shocked, when she reached the bathroom. The toilet bowl was black, looked as though it had never been cleaned, and it stank even worse than anywhere else. Pulling on her latex gloves, she dropped the lid over it and reached across the filthy sink for the window latch.

She almost ran out of the bathroom and slammed the door behind her, hoping to shut out at least some of the stench, but most of it still lingered.

Ava made her way into the first bedroom and stood for a moment, staring around at the unmade bed, the sheets and blankets which were stiff with dirt and something else she didn't want to look at too closely.

But she recognised this room immediately

and a wave of sickness forced its way up to her throat. There was that great, four poster bed. This was the room; this was where it happened.

There was an old fashioned dressing table, dating from about the 1940s, with a triple mirror covered in dust and scarred with black spots. On the table surface were a few pots of cream and a brush and mirror set, the old-fashioned kind with a fancy back. Ava unscrewed the lid of one of the pots, pulling at it with all her strength, then lifted her blouse to cover it and get a better grip. She surmised that it had been years since the container had been opened, if ever. Once the lid was removed, she decided on the latter for it seemed that none of the cream had been used. What was left in the pot was stiff and flaking and the label showed this cream was of a make that had gone out of business many years ago.

Picking up the brush and mirror set, Ava recalled that Gran had one of these, but it was in much better condition and had been well looked after. This set she was now holding had a cracked mirror and the backs were coming away from their plastic covering. Not something Ava wanted to keep; she tossed them both into the dustbin bag, along with the pots of cream and the screwed up tissues that were still scattered over the surface.

The silver photograph frame caught her eye.

It, too, was covered in grime and tarnished as silver is when neglected. She picked it up and rubbed at the glass with her sleeve, found herself staring at a picture which made her heart leap, made her gasp with the shock. It was him! It was her father, not smiling exactly, more smirking.

She stared at it, fought to calm her rapid pulse. The man in the picture was one she had once loved, a man who terrified her. That feeling of betrayal rose up again, that knowledge that she could no longer trust this man she had once loved.

He was older even than she remembered, his thinning hair grey, his face wrinkled, his chin sagging. She remembered clearly now, being moved to this 'grown up' room, to this 'grown up' bed and she remembered what had happened here.

Picking up the heavy frame, she threw it across the room where it bounced against the wall and broke into small pieces as it landed on the floor.

She swept the rest of the tissues onto the floor then stopped and stared at the blonde haired doll which sat leaning against the mirror. It was a teenage doll, with plastic breasts, a bit like Barbie but of a different and cheaper make. She hated that doll, loathed it with all her soul, but she had no idea why.

Picking it up by its hair, she tossed it into the rubbish bag. The house clearance people could have the rest, if they wanted it. She doubted they would, but the dressing table might be worth something. Old stuff like that was becoming more fashionable, although Ava would never understand why. It was really ugly to her eyes, as ugly as the enormous wardrobe which stood against the other wall, looming over her like some eyeless ogre.

She approached it hesitantly and gripped the handle of the wardrobe door, gripped it hard as she half expected a cascade of rubbish to tumble out on her. It didn't, but even so she fell back and landed on the unmade bed.

She could do nothing but stare in horror. Inside the wardrobe were more suitcases, brown, stiff, cracked and old like the first one she'd found downstairs. There were about six of them, all the same size, designed for small items probably. The handle of each case looked as though it might come off, one of them *had* come off, and every one was thick with dust.

How long she sat stiffly on the edge of that bed, she could not have said. All she knew was that she couldn't move, that she was terrified of opening those cases. But she had to open them; there was no one who could take this task from her, no one who could share the secrets that were tumbling out of every cupboard and drawer.

Yet she had no idea what those secrets were; there was no clue among the ancient bills and receipts, no clue even among the photographs of smiling children, little girls with ribbons and slides in their hair, black and white pictures from some sixty years ago. Why should any of that frighten her?

Pushing back the memories that were trying to force themselves to the forefront of her mind, she knew she had only two choices: open those cases herself or take them outside and put a match to them. Whichever option she chose, it would take more courage than she had ever needed before.

She dragged out the first case and heaved it onto the bed, unlatched the catches and stared into it, not wanting to go further. Just seeing the top layer was enough to tell her this case contained more pictures, more little girls. But she had to look deeper, that was necessary; if she didn't, she would always wonder. And those smiling faces would follow her into sleep.

There was nothing to be afraid of, just pictures of little girls, fully dressed most of them, some on a beach with their old fashioned swim suits, shading their eyes from the sun. The suits were smocked, probably cotton and not very waterproof. Did children really wear those? She remembered Gran telling her that, as a child, she had once had a swimsuit her own mother had knitted. Unimaginable, a swimsuit made like that; it would have stretched alarmingly once it was wet.

Ava plunged her hands into the case and briefly flicked through some of the pictures. There were about a hundred in here, just like the case downstairs and now she wondered why it was down there and not up here with the others. But that case had contained pictures of her mother, many pictures of her. She must have been sitting there, admiring them, perhaps remembering how she was corrupted by a family friend, a man old enough to be her father, possibly her grandfather.

Ava shuddered, closed the case and started on the next one. They were all the same, except that some of them had other children in them as well. Some were taken in a playground and she realised that these later pictures had been taken with a long range lens, the tool of stalkers and perverts.

But anyone seeing those earlier pictures would believe they were taken by an amateur photographer, getting in some practice. Ava knew better, knew that the photographer was obsessed with little girls, turned on by them.

Quickly, she opened the last case. This was the one that would be up to date, that should stop twelve years ago when he died and not before time. Unless Shirley had carried on stalking and photographing children, they would stop there and the kids in those pictures would be grown up by now. *If they had a chance to grow up.*

This case was in better condition than the others, more modern too. It was made of a canvas material, dark blue and with a zip fastening. Ava heaved it onto the bed and steeled herself to open it.

So far the pictures had been just cute, if you liked children, nothing sinister about them, nothing at all. She wondered if she was imagining the worst, making mountains out of molehills.

It wasn't locked. Had she expected it to be? The others weren't locked, there was no way to lock those old fashioned cases, so why should this one be?

She pulled the zipper all the way round, flung the lid open and came face to face with her own image. In colour, the best quality and she was smiling, just like the others. She was about six and, thinking hard, she remembered this photograph. She was sitting at the picnic table outside, except it was new then or at least well kept. Now it was rotting and grey but then, in this photo, it was smart.

She was grinning into the camera and now she heard an echo of his voice: "that's wonderful, Ava. You are so pretty."

There was nothing sinister about the words, or the voice, not then. It was only now that she felt the dread of them and as she looked closer at the background of the photograph, she saw on that picnic table the very edge of a birthday cake. Beside it were some birthday cards and one of them showed a big number 6 in silver lettering.

Yes, she was smiling; it was the last time she had until Gran took her away, until she had grown up and met Ryan.

What Ava wanted was to run from this damned house and never come back, but finding this picture had made her even more suspicious of the others. She had to finish, she had to go through with it, even if she ended putting a match to it after all. She had to know.

Wanting to sit, she grimaced at the filthy bedcovers and looked about the room. Buried beneath a pile of dirty clothes, was a white painted wicker chair. She tossed the dirty clothing onto the floor and kicked it out of the way, pulled the chair up closer to the bed so she could reach the suitcase.

There weren't nearly so many pictures in this

one, only about twenty or so, which gave Ava a chance to look at all of them. There were a few more of her, but she wasn't smiling, not in these others. These were taken in that enormous, sunken bath and she was naked, trying to hide herself from the intrusive camera.

She had no memory of these being taken, had no memory at all of what happened after that first night and she was thankful for that. There were a couple of others who looked vaguely familiar, but then she stopped and stared at these last few.

Ava had seen that face before, seen it so often, heard about this girl so often and in so much detail, she felt she had known her all her life. She knew that face, it was on nearly every wall in the house of Ryan's parents.

CHAPTER ELEVEN

Melanie. Ryan's sister, a little girl who had haunted Ava since the day she fell in love with him. For that was the day he told her, wasn't it? That was the day he shared his greatest heartache with her and by so doing, showed her just how much he loved and trusted her.

Not many people knew that Ryan suffered as well; he didn't tell many about his missing sister. In fact, Ava had never known him to tell anyone. Certainly nobody at his workplace had any idea that one of the little girls who went missing locally was his sister. He didn't want their pity and he felt strongly that the heartache belonged to his parents, not to him. Ava couldn't agree with that, but it was his pain to keep, not hers.

She wasn't the only one, though, was she? Melanie was not the only child who had gone missing that year from villages around here. Sorting through this last suitcase, Ava began to take notice, to see if any of the others matched those images the local newspaper had shown, only last week. There was only one, at least in this suitcase, one whose picture had been among those in the paper. But there was Melanie and now here was her picture.

She was on a bench on one of the many

commons in the city, an ice cream cone in her hand and a huge smile on her face. Now Ava looked more closely, just as she had done with the one of herself sitting beside that birthday cake. What she saw was the very edge of a carousel; this was Midsummer Common, where every year a travelling fair arrived and stayed for a few days. It was one of the biggest travelling fairs in the country, most of the travelling fairs from all over who came here to make up this great adventure.

Ava had loved this fair when she was a child and to see Melanie there sent a chill through her and brought back another memory of that little child who had been taken and tortured by Hindley and Brady. She had been abducted from a fairground and never seen again.

Ava slammed the case shut and shoved it back in the wardrobe. She could take no more, not today. She felt that she was choking, that her heart had risen up and got itself stuck in her throat.

She blinked back the tears as she went round the house shutting the windows. She wanted no one to break in here and find...what? Photographs? Innocent photographs? They might well appear innocent, but Ava knew better.

Driving home, Ava thought about her

discovery, trying to keep her mind on the road. Luckily the traffic was light and she arrived in one piece and without causing problems to anyone else.

She made coffee, sat in the silent living room and thought about all those pictures; he must have gone round with a camera, photographing any little girl who took his fancy and what? Did he follow them home? Follow them to school? Or perhaps he knew where he took the pictures so he could find them again.

But Melanie had been abducted, so had that other child and she couldn't help but wonder how many more. He couldn't have kidnapped all the children he had photographed, could he? The worst pervert in the world couldn't have lived long enough to do that.

She wondered how coherent her mother was, whether she could tell her anything, but she doubted it. Her mind had gone, if it had ever been there. It seemed he had followed Shirley for years, stalked her, made friends with her parents and groomed her until she was totally his, completely enthralled.

He was a handsome man at one time, handsome enough to tempt a young girl just coming up to her difficult teenage years. Ava remembered being that age herself, how she had hankered after several good looking actors and singers. She might have been tempted herself.

No, she was making excuses for her now. She was her mother! It was her job to protect her child, not hand her over to a father who would steal her innocence for his own perverted pleasure.

A parade of smiling faces danced before her eyes when she closed them. She thought she knew what had happened. Gran had taken her away from him so he had satisfied himself with photographs and fantasies of these other girls.

That's what these photographs must be about, but there were so many of them. Was it a coincidence then that Melanie's picture was among them, and that other little girl. What was her name? Alice, that was it.

Perhaps someone had noticed him taking pictures and thought it would be safe to take these two children, that if things went wrong, he might be able to blame the stranger with the camera.

It was rational, wasn't it? But Ava couldn't quite convince herself of that, not when she knew better. Every time she tried to find an innocent motive for the photographs, that other one loomed up, an image of herself in that huge bath. But was that innocent, too? Ava didn't think so. Even now, although she couldn't really remember the exact incident, she did recall a sense of deep dread when she had tried to enter that bathroom and a sense of terror when she caught the scent of sandalwood.

And the question which pounded in her brain, getting louder and louder and demanding to be heard, was, should she tell Ryan? What should she tell him, that she had found photographs of his missing sister in a suitcase in her parents' house? Was it fair to give him hope when it could be nothing more than a picture, nothing more sinister than that? It might not be enough to lead to Melanie's whereabouts at all and then what? He would have told Liz and Joe and they would all have been hoping for some closure and been disappointed again.

Closure. God, how she hated that word!

***

"You're very quiet tonight," Ryan remarked as he sat beside her. He put his arm around her and she felt herself drawing away. "What's wrong?"

She shook her head.

"Nothing," she lied. "I'm just thinking about going back to work next week. I've got used to being lazy."

I can't tell him!

Ava had been worrying about it all day,

wondering whether she should tell him what she had found. But what had she found? A photograph, a picture that could mean nothing. Among the hundreds, possibly over a thousand pictures in that house, it wasn't so very unlikely that two of them were of children who had been abducted and never seen again.

Telling Ryan would only upset him and for what? There was no reason to tell him, none at all. But if it was so innocent, there was no reason not to tell him.

"Do you think you'll be finished at the house before you go back?" he asked.

"I hope so. The only thing of value I've found so far has been that dinner service. I took it to the Antique shop in the High Street to be valued. I need to go back and see what he thinks." She moved closer to him and hugged him. "I don't think there'll be much else."

"Then we'll get the house clearance people in; get rid of it all."

"No," she said, a little too quickly. "I need to make sure, for my own peace of mind."

"You've changed your tune. You were all for getting it cleared and I was the one who wanted to explore. What's changed your mind? Anything special?"

This was her chance to tell him, wasn't it? But the words refused to form in her mind, refused to leave her lips. Once out there, once said, there'd be no way to unsay them.

"No," she finally answered. "I just think if the dinner service is worth a bit, there might well be more stuff that's been neglected and forgotten."

It was a lie, and she hated lying to him. It was not what their relationship was based on, not what either of them wanted.

This is her fault! That bloody woman came into our lives and now she's chiselling away at them, destroying what we had.

Shirley Fisher was like an ugly malignant tumour which couldn't be cut out.

Ryan held her closer, kissed her forehead and she snuggled against him, felt his warmth comforting her. This whole business had forged a wedge between them, a wedge she couldn't explain to him and one he knew nothing about.

They had no secrets before, none at all. All right she hadn't told him her mother still lived, but then she'd never really told him she was dead. She told him she didn't have a mother, which wasn't the same thing at all, and as far as she was concerned it was the truth. Now she was keeping things from him, like seven suitcases full of photographs of little girls, like one of those little girls being his missing sister.

No, she wouldn't tell him. Not yet, not until she had found out more. If there was more to find out.

***

It was raining heavily the following day and a sense of urgency was creeping in. She didn't have much longer to get this done and that damned social worker was pestering her again, wanting to know if she'd put the house on the market yet.

Put it on the market? She'd barely made a dent in the sorting out.

So this day, she opened the gate in the pouring rain, drove through and left the gate open. She wasn't getting drenched a second time and while she was there, no one would be breaking in.

But the rain hadn't deterred Mrs Nosy Cheryl, who was waiting when Ava got out of the car. She must have run to follow her in; what was wrong with the woman?

"Terrible weather, isn't it?" she asked.

Stating the bleeding obvious.

Ava locked her car, then turned to face Cheryl. The woman was wearing a Barbour coat, waxed and with a hood, so no rain was getting inside that. She had pasted a false smile onto her immaculately made up face and now stood waiting for an answer.

But there was no answer to give. Yes, it was

terrible weather; any idiot could see that so why mention it? It was just a ruse to start a conversation and maybe get herself invited inside out of the cold and rain. She would be very disappointed.

"How's it going?" Cheryl said, obviously abandoning the idea that she might get a reply. "I've seen you here nearly every day. I did wonder if I should offer to help, but I didn't want to intrude." Again she waited for a reply. At last she shrugged. "Anyway, the offer's there if you should need it. You know where I am."

Both women stood in the driveway of Primrose Cottage, both getting very wet. Ava was probably getting wetter than Cheryl, since the latter had the expensive waxed coat while Ava only had a showerproof jacket but that inconvenience was not going to make her invite the woman in or accept her help.

What would she make of the suitcases filled with little girls' pictures? How long would it take her to spread her opinion as fact all over the town?

Ava wondered fleetingly if she was doing Cheryl an injustice, if perhaps she really did want to help and was really concerned, but she doubted it. She glanced across the road at Cheryl's house, at the hanging baskets, carefully preserved, at the climbing roses, the immaculately cut grass, the modern windows and doors. Cheryl was dressed and made up as though she were about to make a film or pose for a photoshoot.

No, she was doing her no injustice. This woman would have no reason to want to get inside Primrose Cottage, other than to find out what was in there. That, she would never do.

"I'm sorry, Cheryl," she said at last. She wanted to address her more formally, as Mrs, but in truth she had forgotten her surname. "I'm sure you mean well, but this is something I need to do on my own. You understand."

She couldn't really argue with that but she smiled a little then nodded and turned away, hurried through the gate and back to the warmth of her own house, while Ava went inside Primrose Cottage to see what else might be hiding there, waiting to assault her.

A little smile lingered about her mouth; at least the neighbour had given her that much. Ava felt a little sorry for Cheryl; to be so interested in the business of her neighbours, she must have a very shallow existence. But that was unfair. If she lived in this road or one like it, and there was a mysterious woman living in an equally mysterious house at the end of the road, one that was rapidly falling to bits, she would likely be just as intrigued.

The gloomy weather made the inside house even more grim than usual. The sunlight struggling to force its way through grimy windows and Ava immediately switched on the light. It did little to alleviate the gloom, but still, she made her way upstairs.

All she wanted now was to get it over with. She'd done what she could in the first bedroom, thinking perhaps it would be best to put a match to the suitcases and their contents. There was no point in telling Ryan that his sister's photograph was among them; probably her father had taken hundreds of them and it was just a coincidence that those two children had gone missing.

In the second bedroom was another double bed, this one smaller, but no other furniture except a bedside cabinet. The bed stank, just as the first bed had, and at the window hung dark purple curtains which were drawn closed, making the place even darker.

There was another framed picture standing on the surface of the small bedside cabinet. It was her father, to be sure, but in this picture he was much, much younger, confirming her earlier assumption that he was a handsome man.

Thinking about the other photo of him, on that cluttered dressing table, she realised all at once that those pots of cream were not face cream at all, but something much more intimate.

She shuddered, fought back a scream and fled.

The other two bedrooms were empty apart from some fluff and dust on the floorboards and a dead and decomposed mouse in the corner of the first one. No curtains in those rooms, just grimy windows.

There wasn't much to be seen through the dirt, but she pressed her face close and peered through at the garden. All she could see were trees, fruit trees mostly, and the very tip of that shed she had played in as a child, a shed someone had fitted out as a little playhouse.

No, nothing more scary in these rooms than a dead mouse. That was a relief. At least there were no more suitcases to frighten Ava, but the next set of stairs led to the attic. One roof window on which the rain hammered was the only place that any light could come through. Ava looked around until she found a light switch, which lit up the centre and left shadows in the corners. Ava's heart skipped a beat; among those shadows she could see more suitcases.

***

She needed a torch, needed to see more of those corners. She went down the narrow staircase, then the main staircase and rummaged about in the kitchen drawer until she found one which, thankfully, still worked. It wasn't very bright, but enough for her to see into those corners.

There were six of them, some brown, some dark blue and very dirty and these cases were bigger than the others.

Not more photographs! Please, God, not more photographs!

Ava had got to the point where she was just bewildered. She knew what had happened to her in this house, she remembered, although not clearly. She had no desire for the memory to be more lucid, but now she was puzzled as to why her father would have taken all these photographs. And had nobody wondered what he was doing, a strange man following little girls around with a camera?

It wasn't until after the Moors Murders that parents realised it wasn't safe to let their children wander about alone, even in their own home towns. It wasn't till then they realised that evil was lurking, waiting to pounce.

She yanked on the handle of the first case and felt it come away in her hand. She tossed it under the eaves and pulled at the case, dragged it across the dust covered floor and pushed it over onto its base.

Snapping at the catches, she geared herself for

more photographs, hundreds of them, but there were no more. What Ava found made her collapse back onto the floor, covering her mouth to trap an escaping scream, and stare incredulously at the small grey skull that stared back at her from empty eye sockets.

CHAPTER TWELVE

Ava had no idea if she had locked the door. She pointed the remote control at her car and pressed the button as she ran, jumped into the driver's seat and started the engine. Halfway to the gates, she realised she had to go back, had to be sure the house was locked up tight so no nosy Cheryls could find their way inside.

Shaking as she approached the house, afraid some horror would leap out at her, she managed to keep her hand still enough to shove the key into the lock and turn it. Once more she fled, jumped into her car and sat for a moment, trembling so much her vision was impaired.

It was too late now, wasn't it? Far too late. No longer was the decision hers; she would have to go to the police, have to let them find the remains, the photographs and everything else. Have to let them find Melanie.

What would happen, when they found Melanie, when they found those pictures? Ryan would know she knew about them, knew what had happened to his sister and said nothing. He would never understand that she was afraid to tell him, afraid to have him know that it was her father who had stolen that little girl away and destroyed his parents' lives, caused them all so much misery.

That would be the end, the end of the greatest love affair Ava could ever have dreamed of, the end of his love for her. For how could he love her, knowing where she came from?

She didn't realise she was resting her head on the steering wheel until she was wrenched out of her thoughts by a loud knocking on the side window. She jumped, her heart hammered, nearly leapt into her throat to choke her. Reluctantly she steeled herself to look up, expecting to see a rotting skull staring back at her. It was Cheryl.

"Are you all right?" she asked. "You've been sitting there for half an hour."

And you didn't miss a minute of it, did you?

"Yes," Ava managed to mumble. "I am fine."

"I suppose it is upsetting, going through all Mum's stuff like that. It must bring back some memories."

Yes, too many memories. If there was one thing Ava hated it was people talking about someone else's mother as though she were hers. Calling her 'Mum' instead of 'your mum' or saying 'Gran' not 'your gran' as someone did at her funeral. It was pathetic.

"Excuse me," Ava said at last. The engine was still running so she pushed down the clutch pedal and slipped the gear lever into first. "I have to go."

"Are you sure you don't want a coffee? You don't look well."

"Just a headache."

Ava drove away, slowly so as not to run over her unwelcome visitor and picked up speed as she got through the gates and into the road. She glanced at the clock on the dashboard; it was still early and there was somewhere she need to go before it got too late.

***

The nursing home looked even more expensive than it had the last time Ava was here. Of course, she hadn't really taken too much notice before; she was too concerned with what Ryan might be thinking, whether he'd blame her for the woman being found wandering about a motorway.

Or perhaps it was just that now she'd had a chance to get used to her past rearing up and leaving her present in tatters.

"I want to see Mrs Shirley Fisher," she told the receptionist. "I was told by someone that she might be more coherent in the morning."

The young woman smiled and nodded her blonde head.

"That's right. I think Mrs Fisher is quite

chirpy this morning. Are you her daughter?"

Ava wanted to scream *No!* She didn't want to be connected with her in any way, but she had little choice. She nodded.

"I'll take you," said the receptionist.

She led the way along deeply carpeted galleries with windows which looked out at the landscaped grounds. There was a lake in the distance on which the sun shone and swans glided along in pairs.

Ava bit her lip to keep from protesting. Her mother did not deserve to be in a place like this, she deserved nothing so sumptuous, so beautiful. But she wouldn't be here for long, would she? Not now the police would be crawling all over Primrose Cottage. No way to put it up for sale now, no way to release the money to pay for this place. Shirley would have to move into a cheap, state run home. Ava smiled; at least there was a silver lining to this whole, awful mess.

At last they came to a room where a grey haired woman sat and looked out at the horses grazing in a paddock opposite.

"Shirley," the receptionist said in that annoyingly chirpy voice. "We have a visitor. Your daughter's come to see you. Isn't that nice?"

How patronising. Ava thought that if she ever

got so that people thought they could talk to her like that, she'd kill herself.

Shirley turned her head slowly, but she didn't try to get up. She scowled, her mouth turned down, her frown deepened and there was hatred in her faded eyes.

"It was your fault!" She tried to shout but her voice wasn't up to it. "All those others, they were all your fault."

Ava's eyes filled with tears despite her best efforts. She knew she was not to blame; how could she be? She was only a child.

Now the old woman was heaving herself to her feet, clutching onto the arms of the chair, then moving to hold the walking frame which waited nearby. She stood, leaning her full weight on the frame, bent almost double. Ava noticed for the first time that she was still wearing her nightdress, covered with a crocheted bed jacket of the type seen years ago.

"Now then, Shirley," the receptionist piped up. "You know you don't mean that."

God, what an irritating girl and what an irritating voice!

Shirley turned her hate filled eyes on the bouncy receptionist and sneered.

"Piss off!" she said. "This is none of your business."

The blonde girl caught her breath and blinked back tears. She meant well, obviously, and wasn't expecting that. Ava couldn't imagine why, since with all the old folk she had to deal with, she must have annoyed more than one before this.

She touched Ava's arm.

"I think perhaps we'd better come back another time," she said.

"You go," Ava said. "You don't get paid enough to have to put up with the likes of her."

"I don't think it's really safe to leave you here alone with her," she replied.

Then she stepped backwards and pressed a button on the wall, a red button marked 'for emergency use only'. Soon they were joined by two nurses, one male and one female, who wanted to know what the emergency was.

But Shirley hadn't finished.

"If you hadn't told that interfering old cow, he would never have needed anyone else. What do you think we had you for?"

That was enough. Ava could no longer keep the tears inside and she ran, out of the room, along the fancy corridor and out of the building, back to her car.

The police station; that's where she needed to go. She should have done it days ago, when she first found those photographs. *Is every damned traffic light red today?*

Shaking so much she could barely keep her

foot from jumping on the clutch pedal, Ava shot off into the High Street. There was a flash of light in her rear windscreen, enough to tell her she'd been caught by a speed camera. That would mean three points on her licence, but it could take it. Probably put the insurance premium up, though.

She pulled to a sharp stop outside an old, pre-war building with peeling blue paint and a wrought iron arm where once hung the lantern showing the police sign. The Blue Lantern; they'd named a film that once, hadn't they? And why the hell was she even thinking about that now? And what had they done with the police station?

She leaned over the steering wheel and squeezed her eyes shut, tried to clear her mind. They'd closed it, hadn't they? Last year, they'd closed this quaint old police station, where the local copper knew everyone and everything. Now if someone wanted the police, they had to go all the way into Cambridge. Why hadn't she remembered that?

She had to calm herself before she went any further or she'd be getting more speeding tickets, more points on her licence. *Pull yourself together, Ava! You have to tell them about the photographs and the...*

The photographs! They'd find the ones of Melanie and Ryan would want to know why she hadn't told him about them before. Her mother had blamed her, for Melanie and the others. Ryan might also blame her.

An idea occurred to her, an obscure idea that meant she'd have to return to that damned house, but it was the only way, the only way to keep him.

She drove to a side street where she could reverse, turned the car around and headed back to Primrose Cottage. Today the name seemed even sillier; it should be called The House of Usher or perhaps Hill House, something out of one of those old horror films.

There was only one way to remain innocent in all of this and she only hoped she could carry it off.

***

Ava couldn't remember the drive, couldn't recall any of it. Cheryl's curtains twitched as she drove passed, probably wondering why she was back so soon. She'd be there soon, poking her head in the car window, poking her nose into Ava's business. Ava knew she wasn't behaving like a rational person, so the neighbour would be sure to want to know why. She'd pretend to be concerned, of course, but Ava knew an act when she saw one.

She wouldn't mind betting Cheryl wasn't the only neighbour interested in the goings on at Primrose Cottage, but she was the only one ill mannered enough to show herself.

In her hurry to leave earlier, she'd left the gates open so now she had only to drive through them and stop outside the front door. She got out of the car and walked back to shut those gates behind her, before any nosy neighbours came to see what was what.

She glanced up at the sky; good thing the sun had come out, no rain to put out the fire she intended to light.

She opened every suitcase in the wardrobe, dragging the heavier ones across the dusty floor, and sorted through them till she found all the ones of Melanie. There she was, her happy, smiling little face in shots of black and white and colour, in places all over the district that Ava recognised. There was even one on her local green, outside the public house where they had some children's swings.

Then there was one she hadn't seen before. This one was taken in the garden of this house and in it she was wearing Ava's dress. She stopped and stared at that one, her eyes filling with tears when she remembered how sad she'd been when Gran had taken her away from here and left behind her favourite dress and her Bugs

Bunny.

Almost reluctantly she added the picture to the others of Melanie and stood up from the floor. Her jeans were filthy, covered in dust, her hands were dirty but she didn't bother washing them now. Ava hated being dirty, but it would wait.

In the kitchen she found the box of matches she'd seen before and she took them with her into the garden, tossed the photographs into the incinerator. She saved one to set the lighted match to then carefully placed it with the others, stood and watched them burn.

A dart of pain touched her heart as she watched, as she saw that happy, pretty face tearing itself apart with every flame that touched it. She had to be sure they were all completely destroyed before she left, before she found her way to the new police station.

Ashes. Hot ashes. Why hadn't she thought of that before? She couldn't go to the police now; they'd find the hot ashes in the incinerator and know she'd burned something. *Damn! Is it worth praying for rain? It rained yesterday.*

Perhaps she could soak these ashes and hope the police thought they were there before the rain. It was all she could do now. She shivered as she made her way back to the house but stopped partway across the lawn; there was that radio again. Ava looked about, tried to see passed the trees that surrounded the huge garden, but it was impossible.

Inside the house, she went upstairs to the back bedroom and looked out. From here she could see across this garden as well as the neighbouring ones. This one was a lot bigger than she'd thought and there was a row of trees she had assumed was against the back fence. But it wasn't; there were more sheds, some of them enormous, more like summerhouses behind those trees. She could just make out the pitched roofs in the distance.

Ava wondered what horrors she might find in there. She'd leave that to the police and if there were more photographs of Ryan's little sister, she could honestly say she knew nothing about them.

She still couldn't see any neighbouring properties close enough to have an audible radio playing. But she saw something else that sent a shiver through her; there beside the trees were three little mounds with crosses. Graves, that was obvious, but whose? They couldn't be victims, could they? They wouldn't be so obvious if they were victims. Ava felt sure they must be the remains of pets, perhaps cats or dogs who had passed away. It seemed unlikely; Ava recalled asking for a dog and her mother refusing. Gran had got her a little dog, but that was later.

She would have to go outside and look at those little graves before she called in the police. She knew she'd have to do it, have to force herself to do it.

And that's when it began to rain.

***

Ava was annoyed to discover she couldn't simply open the door and walk into the new police station. There was a panel on the wall where official people could enter a number. Next to that was a buzzer thing and Ava pressed it and waited.

Nobody answered at first and she stood outside, observing the traffic and the people walking passed. She'd come to report a serial killer and they kept her waiting all this time. And how was she going to tell this machine on the wall about it?

At last, a voice came out of the intercom, making her jump.

"Can I help you, Madam?"

"Yes. Can you let me in, please."

"When you tell me your business here."

Ava swallowed; she was getting angry now. This was important, had given her nightmares for days yet he wouldn't let her in. Perhaps she should go back to her car and phone the emergency number on her mobile phone. Perhaps she should have done that in the first place.

"Are you still there, Madam?" came the voice.

Ava knew they were watching her on a video screen and knew damned well she was still here.

"I want to report a murder," she said at last. "Several murders in fact. Now will you let me in?"

***

They were quick to attach police crime scene tape to the gates of Primrose Cottage, quick to tell Ava she couldn't go in. A bit daft, after she'd spent days inside the house, going over everything.

The inspector in charge told her to go home, that he would visit later to take her statement. That meant she'd have to explain it all to Ryan before he got there and that meant, in turn, that she'd have to phone him at work and get him home.

She hated doing that. He was usually in the middle of some major project or other, but it seemed this might be more important.

"But, please, Inspector," she said. "Can you

just look at the end of the garden? Tell me those three little graves are animals. Please."

"I can't disturb them," he answered. "Not until we've finished in the house."

"I don't want you to disturb them," she said. "I just want to know if there are any inscriptions on the crosses. I didn't quite have the nerve to go and look, not after what I found in the attic."

He gave her a sorrowful look, then nodded slightly. He could see how upset she was, that she wouldn't be able to wait.

"Wait here," he said quietly, touching her arm.

He was gone about five minutes then returned to tell her the crosses had names and dates, three boys' names and dates less than a year apart. All the dates were before Ava was born.

"What do you think they mean?" she asked.

"I can't say, Mrs Kenyon. All I know is, if those babies died legally, they would be in a churchyard, not at the bottom of the garden."

Boys! Baby boys! Who the hell were they?

Ava had just got in and had time to put the kettle on when the phone rang. It was that damned social worker, wanting to know how the house situation was going. That's what she called it; the house situation.

"I'm afraid it won't be going up for sale just

yet," said Ava and felt a little dart of satisfaction.

"But your mother cannot stay at Lawston Manor for much longer without paying. You must realise that if funds aren't available soon, she'll have to be moved to a less expensive facility."

So what?

"That can't be helped, I'm afraid," said Ava.

"What's the hold up?"

The tone of her voice changed abruptly from sweet and cloying to irritated. Ava knew that first tone was insincere.

"The hold up is that several skeletons have been discovered in the attic."

Mrs Carlton laughed, apparently thinking that Ava was making some sort of dark joke.

"I did hear that you visited your mother this morning," she said. *That didn't take long.* "I heard Mrs Fisher was rambling. Such a shame, when we all thought she was more coherent in the mornings."

"She was coherent," said Ava, but she didn't want to go into details, not to this woman. "The fact is that I have found the remains of several children in the attics of the house. I have informed the police; they've cordoned off the place and won't let anyone in. It looks like it could be a while before the house can be sold."

The silence from the other end of the line was

almost audible.

"You're not joking, are you?" said Mrs Carlton.

"I would hardly joke about the remains of children."

The social worker exhaled a loud sigh.

"Then your mother will have to be moved," she said. "Unless you can pay her fees yourself?"

It was obviously a question; Ava could hear it in her tone. She laughed at that. The very idea that she might be persuaded to dip into their precious savings, or the money that Gran had left her, to keep an evil-minded murderer in luxury, was laughable.

"No," she replied. "We won't be doing that."

"I thought you inherited quite a bit from your mother's mother," said Mrs Carlton. "She would surely want her own daughter to benefit, wouldn't she?"

How did she know about that?

"If that were the case, she'd have left everything to her, not me," said Ava. "Now, I need to phone my husband and get him to come home before the police arrive to take a statement from me. I don't want him walking into the middle of it."

***

They sat together on the sofa, Ryan's warm hands in Ava's, while she told him what she had discovered that day in the attics of Primrose Cottage. She told him nothing else; she couldn't bring herself to tell him anything else. Describing the sight that had reared up to meet her when she unlatched that suitcase brought an ache to her throat and tears to her eyes for the first time. She'd felt nothing but horror at the time, no sympathy for those dead children.

Children? How did she know there were children? The truth was, she didn't, not for certain but there was more than one skull in that suitcase, more than two legs, two arms and Ava had been too afraid to look further. Besides, had she looked closer, she would have been tampering with evidence. At least that's what she told herself.

"Do you think she's there?" Ryan whispered hoarsely.

Ava knew at once who he was talking about and she knew, too, that her answer should be 'yes' but she just couldn't say it. Instead, she leaned closer and held him tightly. The guilt started then, the guilt for burning those photographs and not telling him his sister's was among them.

I shouldn't have done that; that was a big mistake and now I can't undo it. Now I have to live with it and keep my mouth shut.

"I don't know," she lied. "It's possible. But please, don't tell your mother; not yet. No point getting her hopes up."

"You're right."

He held her close, kissed the top of her head and she could feel his heart beating faster, knew he was deciding if it would be good or bad to know that Melanie had been abused and murdered by his wife's father.

"I suppose this is why your gran took you away," Ryan said.

"It must have been. I don't remember; I don't remember anything."

"Just as well," Ryan said. "We'll soon know more than we ever wanted to."

But Ava knew this was the end; the end of a wonderful marriage to a wonderful man, the end of a love she never expected to have. She'd always thought she didn't deserve him and now she knew why.

CHAPTER THIRTEEN

"Is this your sister, Sir?"

The detective sergeant held in his hand a photograph, one that Ava hadn't seen. She'd gone through all those cases, removed all the pictures of Melanie and burned them, yet here was another.

This one was colour and the girl in the image, although undoubtedly Melanie, was older, possibly even a few years older.

"Where did you find this?" Ava demanded. "I didn't see this one among all the others."

"No," said the sergeant. "It wasn't in one of the cases. We found it in the dark room, in the cellar."

Ava made no reply. She hadn't got as far as looking for the dark room she knew must have been there somewhere.

Ryan was nodding, tears in his eyes as he clasped tightly to Ava's hand and she felt him shiver. She released his hand and wrapped her arm around him, held him close.

"But this girl's older," he said. "She was only seven when she disappeared. This girl must be twelve or thirteen."

"It is true that the remains we've found so far have been of much younger children," said the sergeant. "The ones we've identified were killed almost as soon as they were abducted. Your sister is different."

Ryan glared at the sergeant, his teeth clenching angrily.

"So you're telling me that Melanie suffered for what? Five years or more at the hands of this monster? Is that what you're telling me?"

"I'm not telling you anything yet, Mr Kenyon, and I know this is difficult. But it seems they hung onto this girl for some reason."

"And you don't know what that reason might be?" demanded Ryan. "You can't guess?"

"Yes, of course we can guess," said the sergeant. "But without a coherent witness, we cannot know for sure."

"You've spoken to her?" asked Ava. "You've been to see the old cow?"

The sergeant nodded.

"The inspector has been a couple of times, both in the early morning, but she doesn't remember anything."

"Is that what you think?" said Ava. "I wouldn't be surprised to find she's putting it on. She certainly knew who I was when I went to see her."

The sergeant nodded, flushed pink.

"I did hear about the altercation," he said. "It must have been upsetting for you."

"A little," she replied sarcastically.

"But Melanie," Ryan persisted.

"Yes, Sir. This is the only connection we have so far made with your sister. We have cleared the attics and the rest of the house. We are about to dig up the garden."

"But the graves," said Ava. "What will happen to those?"

"We will examine the remains as best we can to try to determine their identities and the cause of death. We've searched public records but there's no evidence of any births." He smiled kindly. "Don't worry, love," he said. "They'll be given a decent burial."

There was that phrase again: 'a decent burial' as though it mattered. But it did matter, at least to most people. It was only Ava who thought it a waste of time and money. Those little baby boys could be her brothers and she knew they'd be waiting for her in spirit.

That night when Ava climbed into the king size bed beside the husband she adored, she felt an imperceptible distance between them, a distance she couldn't have explained. She reached up and turned out her bedside lamp, he did the same, and she slid across the bed to wrap her arms around him and hold him. But tonight was different, tonight he didn't hold the hand that rested on his waist, didn't turn to kiss her.

"It's over, isn't it?" she said softly.

"What?"

"Us. I knew she'd come between us, I knew she'd destroy everything."

"No," he protested, but didn't turn to comfort her. "I just feel a little bruised, that's all."

Too bruised to hold me. She turned over to face the wall; he did nothing to stop her.

***

Ava wanted another look before the police started to dig up the garden. The tape was still there, telling everyone to keep out, crime scene, but there was nothing else to stop her, not at that time in the morning.

There was a police car parked in the driveway, which gave her pause, but as she crept closer she saw that the officer inside was snoring softly. She wouldn't tell; it was to her advantage.

Ryan had already left when she woke up. It was much too early for him to leave for work, the office wouldn't be open yet, but she knew where he had gone. He'd gone to tell his parents that the police might have found Melanie, found her in the house belonging to his wife's parents. And he didn't want Ava with him.

She'd parked outside the gates, in the road.

The idea was to sneak in unnoticed and she managed that. Even nosy Cheryl's curtains were still safely drawn as Ava drove passed and now she ran around the back of Primrose Cottage and into that enormous back garden.

It was vast, at least three acres, more than half of which were trees. It seemed to go on forever. She hadn't bothered to explore here before; it was the one place in the entire property that she remembered with some sort of pleasure. Before her birthday, she'd spent many happy hours here, playing with her dolls and their little pram, swinging from the one swing that her father had put up specially for her.

Now it hung on rusty chains, the wooden seat split and rotted away. The slide beside it didn't look very safe either, the steps not too sturdy.

Ava stared at it and caught back a sob. The memories were flooding her mind now, memories of playing here, a normal child, her mother calling her in for her dinner, her not wanting to leave her game.

Everything was so ordinary then, before her birthday. She didn't realise at the time that other children went to school; Ava didn't go to school. She didn't know any other children so she had no way of knowing about school, not until Gran took her away and enrolled her in the one close to her.

She was way behind all the other children because nobody had bothered to teach her anything; it wasn't necessary, was it? Not considering what they had planned for her future.

Walking slowly towards the end of the garden, she stopped beside the little graves with their little crosses, each one with a name and a date. Ava took out her phone and punched in the three names, Robert, Alan, David. They all seemed to have been born one after the other in the years before Ava came along. Then she pointed her phone at each grave and took a photograph.

She stood transfixed on those crosses. These little boys were her brothers, at least, she thought they were. When she got home she intended to search public records on the internet to see if she could learn more.

The police didn't find anything; what makes you think you can? That little voice of her conscience was arguing with her again, but that was all right. At least she had someone who knew the truth.

Now she hurried towards the orchard at the end of the garden, towards the summerhouse where she used to play, pretending it was her house, that the dolls were her children. She'd had a whole toy kitchen in that summerhouse, she had a little table and chairs and child sized armchairs.

She just wanted to see it all, just wanted to see if she could grab hold of the only memories she had of when she was innocent, when she was happy.

Now she could see that it was just a shed, big enough for a little girl to play in. At the time it had seemed massive, house sized, but then Ava had been only little herself. The wood was beginning to rot, the door creaked when she opened it, but it was all still there. Her little plastic kitchen stood in the corner, her little armchairs growing a little moss and the red paint was peeling off the table and chairs.

She closed the door and left it all, came back out into the garden, among the fruit trees. There was a new summerhouse now, much, much bigger. This one was like one of those log cabins she'd seen in outdoor furniture places, but it held no memories for her.

As she made her way towards it, she kept her eyes down on the ground to be sure she didn't tread on any rotten apples. The grass was covered in them, where they had fallen off the trees and nobody had bothered to pick them up. There weren't only apples, either; there were plums and some pears, all over ripe and badly bruised.

And there was that bloody radio again. Where was it coming from? There were no neighbours close enough and as Ava drew closer to the summerhouse, the music grew louder. But it couldn't be coming from there. How could it?

There was a light on inside; she could see through the window and as she approached, someone inside turned off that light.

Ava's heart was hammering faster as she gripped the door handle and tried to open the door. It was firmly locked; she moved along and peered through the window. Someone was in there; a young woman was standing on the far side of the room, her fingers on the radio control, and now it went quiet. She must have heard Ava because she turned towards the window, looked scared, her eyes wide and frightened, while Ava wondered who on earth she could be.

She went back to the door and ran her fingers along the top of the frame, searching for a key. There was nothing. She went back to the window.

"Will you open the door, please," she called out.

There was no response, but she could see the girl move back, away from the door, against the wall and she was looking around frantically, probably searching for a weapon.

"It's all right," Ava called out. "I won't hurt you."

Then she saw a large flower pot beneath the window and she lifted it. There was the key, in such an obvious place she wouldn't have thought to look there first. She shoved the key into the lock, afraid now that the frightened young woman would have found herself a weapon and was too afraid not to use it.

Ava opened the door carefully, ready to close it again quickly to protect herself. But the girl just stood there, her back against the wall and she was obviously terrified. Ava, on the other hand, was shocked, shaken, wondering if the strain of the last few days had played tricks with her mind.

The girl who stood there before her was about nineteen years old and she was someone Ava recognised at once.

"Who are you?" the young woman demanded. "Where's my mother?"

CHAPTER FOURTEEN

Dressed in the fashion of some thirty years ago, the girl stood absolutely still, almost rigid, her eyes wide and frightened, her fists clenched. The skirt and tee shirt she was wearing seemed to be old, not just the style, but the garments themselves. The skirt was very flared, had once been white with embroidered flowers all over it.

A memory flashed into Ava's mind, a memory that held Ava's mind locked in the past. It was that skirt. Strange, it was one of the very few things she remembered of her mother, because she had loved that skirt and used to dress up in it whenever she got the chance. It was much too big for her, which made it even better as it came down to her feet and she could pretend to be a fairy princess while wearing it.

But this girl wasn't playing dress up; the skirt fitted her perfectly, as did the plain white tee shirt she wore with it.

"I'm sorry." Ava finally found her voice. "I didn't expect to find anyone here."

"I live here," said the girl. "Where's my mother? I haven't seen her for weeks. What have you done with her?"

Ava had no idea how to answer that question. Her eyes searched rapidly around the room until they came to rest on the colour television set in the corner. It was old, not flat screen like the ones of today, and there was a video player on the shelf underneath it. There was a bookcase beside it with lots of video tapes, not something one saw very often nowadays. No DVDs anywhere to be seen, only video tapes.

In the corner of the vast room was a kitchen of sorts, with a sink and a few cupboards. There was an upright freezer, quite modern, and beside it a smaller fridge and a microwave oven.

"Well?" the girl said impatiently.

She seemed to have found some courage, something that was lacking when Ava first encountered her. The meekness was going now, gradually, although it still lingered a little. She hadn't moved from the spot beside the radio, her back pressed up against the wall, where she had moved to when Ava opened the door.

Opening her mouth to tell the girl that the woman she was asking about was not her mother, Ava felt her tongue almost glued to the roof of her mouth. She couldn't tell her that, could she? She would never be believed. Twelve years was a long time in the life of a child.

But what was she doing here? Why had Shirley kept this one alive? Did the old man want to amuse himself some more? Ava shook her head; it made no sense. But she'd seen his death certificate somewhere among the piles of paper and now the date came back to her. He must have died shortly after Melanie vanished. He died, Shirley didn't have the courage to kill the child herself, so she had kept her. And perhaps she had regretted losing her own little girl and wanting to raise this one. Who knew? Who would ever know? She was certainly in no fit state to tell anyone.

"Melanie?" Ava finally managed to stammer.

"How do you know my name? Who are you?"

I'm your sister-in-law, married to your brother.

But this needed a professional, didn't it? She had no idea what to do, what to say or how to soothe the girl's suspicion.

"My name is Ava," she said softly. "You need to come with me."

Melanie began to shake her head vigorously, her blonde curls cascading about her shoulders, and she looked even more terrified.

"I mustn't leave here," she said. "Mother told me. There are people out there, bad people who want to hurt me."

Ava bit her lip, hard, and her eyes filled with tears. So that's how she'd kept her in this log cabin all these years, by frightening her into thinking this was the only safe place for her.

"Why would anyone want to hurt you?"

Melanie shook her head again, slower this time.

"She wouldn't tell me. She only told me that's why I have to live here, where it's safe. Where is she? Where's my mother?" She turned her head a little, gave a quick glance at the freezer in the corner. "The food's almost gone. She wouldn't leave me like this without seeing her. Not unless …"

Unless she's dead.

Melanie didn't say it, but it was clear that's what she was thinking. Ava reached out and hesitantly took hold of her hand, expecting her to yank it away, but she only glanced down at the two clasped hands, then her eyes met Ava's.

"Is she?" she said. "Is she dead?"

What was there to say to that? Ava desperately wanted to tell her that yes, she was dead and gone, never to be seen again. But that was a lie and was not her place; it could cause the girl more trauma than she'd already suffered.

"The … the woman you've been calling your mother," Ava began, then paused to watch the reaction before going on. "She's not well. She's in a hospital of sorts. You can't stay here."

"But it's not safe. She said people were looking for me."

"They are; they have been for twelve years,

but not to do you harm."

"Why then?" Melanie demanded.

"Because you were stolen from them and they love you."

Ava knew she should say no more, that she should leave it to the professionals, but she couldn't bear to know that Melanie was here, alive and apparently well, but Liz and Joe and Ryan knew nothing. She wanted to put her in the car and take her home to them, now, right now.

Melanie's head spun round suddenly and she pulled her hand away from Ava's to run to the window. There was a noise outside, men's voices. They were close to the other side of the trees; it seemed likely they were digging the garden, starting with the three little boys.

Ava had to persuade Melanie to leave before they got started in earnest.

"Who's that?" Melanie said. "What are they doing? Why are they here?"

"Melanie, please. You must come with me. Do you have a warm coat?"

She turned away, went to a dresser and pulled out a thick cardigan. It was cold outside, getting on for autumn. The cardigan didn't look warm enough. Ava began to take off her own coat.

"Wear this," she said.

"No." She pulled the cardigan away from Ava. "My mother made me this. When I visit her in the hospital, she'll be pleased to know I'm wearing it. I've never really had a chance before."

As Melanie pushed her arms into the knitted jacket, Ava noticed the Marks and Spencer label in the collar, proving that Shirley hadn't knitted it as she had claimed. But she'd never had a chance to wear it before. What did that mean? That she never went outside at all? Ava wasn't about to ask. She pushed her arms back into her coat and turned to see that Melanie was now wearing the bright red, chunky knit cardigan. It was old fashioned but obviously brand new.

"Come on, then," Ava said.

At the door, Melanie stopped, looked at the world outside and took a step back.

"Who is it talking?" she asked.

"They are the police," said Ava.

"The police? What are they doing here? What's happened?"

My God! How can I answer her questions?

She knew the answers, but she couldn't give them to her. She was afraid of the affect they might have on a girl who had lived in this cabin for all the years she could remember. And she had to phone Ryan.

She put her arm around Melanie and tried to

lead her to the door. Again, she stopped.

"I don't think I ought to go out there," she said. "Mother wouldn't like it. She told me I must never go outside without her in case they found me."

"But she didn't explain who 'they' were, did she?"

"She said it would frighten me."

Ava glanced back at the television set in the corner of the room and an idea came to her.

"Don't you ever watch the news on the television?" she asked.

"It doesn't do that," said Melanie. "It's only for playing videos and now Mother got me a DVD player. I'm collecting those now but so far I've only got one. She said she'd get me one every week when she ordered the shopping, but she hasn't been back for ages. She is still alive, isn't she?"

Yes, she bloodywell is! Unfortunately.

"Listen Melanie," said Ava. "We have to leave. I'll take you in my car to see your …" She stopped. She was about to say 'your mother' but then she'd have to explain that she wasn't referring to Shirley. "Come with me, please. I'll look after you."

"I've never been in a car," said Melanie. "I've only seen them on my television. Will you take me to see my mother?"

Yes! But not the one you mean.

How to explain to the police officers who were digging up the garden, still searching the house? Melanie stopped once more when they reached the door and Ava wondered if she might be agoraphobic after spending so much time locked in here. But finally she took that step over the threshold and out into the fresh air.

They walked slowly, passed the police who were digging carefully. Ava didn't want to see what they'd found and she didn't want Melanie to see it either, but they were forced to stop when one of the police officers straightened up and called out to her.

"Mrs Kenyon," he said. "What are you doing? You know you're not supposed to cross the tape, don't you? And who is this?"

Ava desperately wanted to move away from the sight before them, wanted to move Melanie away from the sight before them.

"Can we go closer to the house, officer?" she said. "Then I'll explain."

He nodded, put his shovel down on the grass and led the way while Ava put herself firmly between Melanie and the little graves.

There was a dilapidated garden bench near the house and she sat Melanie down and told her to wait while she spoke to the policeman. She didn't want her to hear; it was too soon for that.

"This is Melanie Kenyon," she told him.

"Kenyon? That's your name. Did you bring her here to have a nose round?"

The man was a uniformed police officer and obviously knew nothing about the investigation; the name meant nothing to him.

"I need to speak to your inspector," she said. "Melanie has been missing for twelve years; he knows all about it. He knows where I live."

He nodded, went back to the dig site where his jacket and his radio waited.

"Come on, Melanie," said Ava. "We'll go to my car. I need to make a phone call."

Melanie laughed, a sound Ava had never expected to ever hear. In all the years she'd known Ryan, known about this girl, she had never expected to hear her voice and certainly not her laugh.

All she knew was that Ryan would be relieved beyond measure to know that she was unharmed and seemed in good spirits. But would that last when they told her who she really was?

She opened the car door and Melanie slipped into the passenger seat. She touched things curiously, opened the glove compartment and looked inside, turned round and looked at the back seats.

Ava opened the driver's door and leaned

down to look inside.

"Are you all right for a minute, while I phone?" she asked.

"Can't I come with you?" Melanie replied. "I've never been inside the house before."

"I'm not going into the house," Ava said. She pulled her smartphone out of her pocket and showed it to her. "I have a phone here."

"Oh!" Melanie cried out loud enough to make Ava jump. "I've seen that on my television. I thought it was science fiction. How can it work without any wires?"

That's something Ava had always wondered herself.

"I don't know, really," she said. "I only know it does."

She smiled indulgently as she closed the door and turned away to lean on the car as she clicked on the first speed dial on the list. How the hell was she going to tell him?

"Hello, darling," came the familiar voice. "Are you okay? Listen, I'm sorry about last night."

Last night. She had forgotten about last night, so much more had happened.

"It's okay," she said. "I understand."

"I'm not sure that you do. You see …"

"It doesn't matter, Ryan," she interrupted him. "I have something more important to tell you."

"Melanie," he whispered hoarsely. "They've found her, haven't they?"

"In a manner of speaking."

"What does that mean?" His voice rose impatiently. "If they haven't found her, I don't want to know about more photographs, more hints that she might have been one of your old man's victims."

Your old man.

Did she imagine the emphasis on that word 'your' or was it really there? She swallowed hard, tried to get the words out.

"You left early," she said. "Did you tell your mum and dad?"

"No. I meant to, but when I got there I realised I didn't have anything to tell them. At least not anything that would make them feel better."

The sound of the horn made her heart jump, made her leap away from the car. She turned to see Melanie, smiling and mouthing 'sorry'.

At least he had taken her advice not to tell his parents anything until they were sure; at least they'd spared them that much. And how would they feel when they found this adult who remembered nothing about them, who thought Shirley Fisher was her mother? Ava did not even try to guess.

"They haven't found Melanie," she said into the phone. "*I* have. She's with me now. Ryan, she's alive."

CHAPTER FIFTEEN

He must have broken every speed limit between his office and Primrose Cottage and he didn't do the tyres any good when he screeched to a stop. Ava glanced at Melanie to see if the noise of skidding brakes had frightened her, but she was still fiddling with the radio when Ryan slammed his door and ran at Ava.

"Where?" he demanded. "Where is she?"

"She's in the car, but listen, you have to be careful. She doesn't remember who she is, only her name and she thinks my mother is hers."

"Then we'll tell her."

"Just like that? I think we ought to wait for the professionals."

"Professionals?" He almost shouted the word and he was shaking his head, looking in the car at the young girl who sat there, dressed in a tatty old tee shirt and knitted jacket, fascinated by all the different knobs on the dashboard.

Then she looked up and Ryan opened the driver's door, stuck his head in. Melanie smiled, a big, wide, welcoming smile which Ava read at once.

"Melanie?" he said. "You remember me, don't you?"

"Wish I did," she said with a big sigh. "I'd

certainly remember a hunk like you."

He withdrew from the car, closed the door and turned back to Ava.

"Haven't you told her anything?" he asked sharply.

"No. Only that it is safe outside the log cabin where she's lived for the past twelve years."

"I wonder why she was kept alive," he muttered, almost to himself.

"Because he died," said Ava. "I think he died the same day he kidnapped her, or shortly after, and Shirley kept her, told her she was her mother."

"She wanted to replace you?"

She didn't like his tone, didn't like it at all. It seemed to her that, like her mother, he was blaming her. His sister would never have gone missing had she kept her father's secrets to herself.

She tried to talk herself out of the notion. How could it be her fault? She was six years old, a terrified child in need of help.

"You stay with her," Ava said. "I'll go and tell your mum and dad that we've found her."

"No, you stay with her. She seems to trust you and if I stay, I think she'll be disappointed to learn that I'm her brother."

It should have been an offhand, sardonic remark, but there was that tone again. She couldn't fight off the niggling little voice in her head that insisted he didn't want her with him. Perhaps he didn't. How was he going to explain that their little girl, who they had mourned, had been kidnapped by his wife's father and held prisoner all these years by his wife's mother. Would they also blame her?

He got back into his car and drove away, more carefully this time, and he passed the police inspector as he reached the end of the road.

The passenger door opened just as the inspector was pulling up behind them; Melanie put one foot outside and looked across the roof of the car at Ava.

"Don't you have any music?" she said.

Ava smiled encouragingly, leaned into the car and switched on the radio, thankful that it worked without the ignition on. This girl seemed so naïve, so unworldly, unaffected by everything. But that had to be an illusion.

She made sure the door was shut fast before she turned to the inspector.

"Where did you find her?" he said. "We searched the whole house."

"She wasn't in the house. In fact, she said she'd never been inside the house but I think she must have been, just doesn't remember. She was living in a summerhouse right down the end of the garden, in the orchard. She thinks Shirley Fisher is her mother."

"What have you told her?"

"Not much. I was waiting for some advice on that, but I don't think my husband or his parents are going to wait. I think I need to try to explain."

He nodded.

"Take her home with you then. I'll have a family liaison officer meet you there."

With a sense of relief, as though she'd been given permission to do what she'd wanted to all along, Ava got in the car, fastened the seat belt around her passenger, and drove toward home.

When they got on the dual carriageway, Ava put her foot down and sped up to the speed limit and beyond.

"Whee!" Melanie squealed, that terrific smile getting wider. "I like this."

"Have you never …?" Ava was about to ask if she was sure she'd never been in a car before, but she stopped, knowing that yes, she had, but she had no memory of it.

"Are we going to see my mother now?" Melanie asked.

"No. At least … I have some things to tell you first, but I don't want to do it while I'm driving. Watch the view; we'll be home soon."

***

Liz and Joe were intently watching the television news when Ryan arrived. He didn't have to see the screen to know what it was about; he could hear it clearly enough. Not sure how to tell them his sister was still alive, he stood for a moment before he showed himself, listening to the report and the silence from his parents.

He should have good news; hell, he did have good news. But after everything, he wasn't sure how they would take it. He knew they'd want to see her straight away, have her home, perhaps even expect her to be their little girl, just an older version of the child who disappeared. How was he to tell them she was no such thing, that she had no memory of them, that she thought Ava's mother was her mother? And how was he to tell them it was his wife's father who had stolen her from them in the first place?

Upstairs, Melanie's bedroom was the same little girl room she had left behind. There were dolls, a pink child's laptop covered in plastic flowers, pink lace hangings from the small four poster bed and a Cindy doll house. Would they think she could just fit back into that background, grow up all over again with the right mother?

From his position he could see the giant photograph of his wedding to Ava, the one where an extra bridesmaid had been added. That bridesmaid had been aged from the photograph Ava's friend had worked with and now Ryan knew how much like his sister it really was.

He swallowed, closed his eyes and took a step into the living room. Liz turned first, her eyes red and swollen; she had already accepted the worst.

"Is it her?" Liz asked. There was a note of panic in her voice; she wanted to know, yet she didn't want the answer. "It is, isn't it?"

"Out with it, boy," said Joe. "We've waited long enough. Don't hold back now. Have they found our girl?"

Ryan swallowed again. In all the years he'd thought about finding his sister alive, he'd never imagined it would be like this.

"Yes, Dad," he said quietly. "They've found her. She's alive."

Liz stared at him, her eyes wide and round, then she leapt to her feet and grabbed his lapels, hung onto him till his collar sank into his neck.

"Say that again," she demanded. "I thought I heard you say she's alive."

"I did, Mum."

He loosened her grip and pulled her into his

arms. Joe was still sitting in front of the television set, his head turned, his eyes fixed on his son.

"Alive?" said Liz. "You mean she's been suffering all these years? Like that poor girl in Austria whose father locked her in the cellar for twenty years? What has he been doing with her? Has he been … " She couldn't say it. "Has she had babies? Is that what he's done?" She paused, her mouth formed a grim line of a hatred Ryan had never seen before. She almost spat the next words: "How could Ava's father be the one?"

He had to hold her up then. He felt her slipping down toward the floor, felt her legs losing strength and he caught her, guided her to the sofa and sat beside her. She seemed to have forgotten that Ava's father died about the same time that Melanie was abducted, so none of that could have happened. Despite this, he decided to humour her.

"We don't know any of that yet, Mum," he said. "We don't think so. It seems likely that the old man kidnapped Melanie, then died before he could do her any harm."

"And his wife kept her? She didn't think perhaps her parents were desperate to know she was safe?"

"It seems that way."

"Ava's mother? She's a mother herself; didn't

she realise? Didn't she have any sympathy for us?"

"It doesn't seem like she was a very good mother, does it? She let him have her own daughter; she colluded in it. That's why Ava hates her so much."

Liz was nodding slowly, her face flushed, her anger growing.

"Let's hope she hasn't inherited her mother's nature."

Ryan moved away from her. He was shocked, more shocked than even the discovery at Primrose Cottage had made him. His mother was the sweetest woman, even keeping her complacent and gentle nature after twelve years of anguish. He had never seen her angry, certainly never seen her vindictive. And she was talking about his wife, the woman he loved.

He knew this whole thing had been a terrible blow, to all of them, but it was hardly Ava's fault. And he should say so, shouldn't he? She was his wife. He should be taking her side, but his mother was too distraught to be arguing with now.

He got to his feet, ready to leave, to go home to that wife, to Ava, who was also distressed by this whole thing.

"Well," Joe said. "Are they bringing her home now, or what?"

"I think Ava's taken her to our place."

Liz leapt to her feet, showing more animation than Ryan could ever remember.

"I don't want her left there," she said. "How can I know she's safe?"

That was it. Ryan could keep quiet no longer.

"That's enough, Mother," he said. "Ava has done nothing to make you think badly of her. Nothing at all. I'll not have you talking about my wife like that."

Liz was glaring at him, sending a look his way that made him shiver. Joe stood, put his arm around his wife.

"Ryan's right, love," he said. "You're just overwrought."

"I'll see what's happening," Ryan said. "The liaison officer was going to see Melanie at ours. We thought that would be a nicer environment than a police station. I'll let you know when you can see her."

"Let us know? Let us know?" Liz yelled, leaving Ryan wondering who this woman could possibly be. "She's our daughter! Don't you think that family have seen enough of her?"

"That family, Mum?"

Ryan shook his head and turned to the front door, but behind him, Liz was putting on her coat, ready to go with him. He couldn't allow that; he was still smarting from her attack on

Ava.

"We'll come with you, son," said Joe. "We just want to see her. You can understand that."

"Of course I can, but you need to wait and see what the liaison officer thinks. Promise?"

They both nodded agreement, but Ryan didn't trust his mother's. He'd never seen her behave like this and to blame Ava for the crimes of her parents was just not the sort of thing he expected of her.

***

The liaison officer was a young, dark haired woman in a smart police uniform and with a permanent smile that Ava suspected might be false. She looked to be too young to be attending a victim of possible child abuse, certainly of kidnapping and imprisonment, albeit comfortable imprisonment.

When she arrived, Melanie was flicking through the channels with the remote control. She hadn't found the news channel yet, which was just as well, and Ava wasn't sure what she would do when she did.

"Melanie, you had your own tv in your place," she said. "What's so fascinating about this one?"

"I never had all this," she said. "My telly only

played the videos and the DVD."

Ava nodded.

"I see. But choose something and watch it, please. It's really irritating to have it keep flicking through all of them."

Melanie looked at her solemnly.

"Sorry," she said.

"Instead of that, why don't you tell me what you remember?"

"I don't understand."

"What do you remember from before you went to live in the log cabin?" Ava said.

"I still don't understand," said Melanie. "I've always lived there." Her voice began to rise a little. "You said we were going to see my mother."

Thankfully, that's when the doorbell rang and Ava opened the door to see the liaison officer waiting on the doorstep. She breathed a sigh of relief and retreated to the kitchen to let the young woman see Melanie in private. Ava was eager to listen, but thought it best to leave them alone.

There was a fresh free range chicken in the refrigerator and she put it in the oven and started to peel potatoes. A nice, roast dinner would be a treat for Melanie. It looked as though she'd had nothing but microwave food for years; what with that and the lack of real sunlight, no wonder she looked so pale.

There was no television in the kitchen. Ava had always refused to have one, always said she didn't intend to spend that much time there. Now she wished she did have one, but wishes wouldn't help so she went upstairs to her bedroom to retrieve the book she was reading from the bedside cabinet.

She was only ten pages into the story when she heard Ryan's key in the door. She also heard voices and knew he'd brought his parents with him. This was going to be a difficult reunion and Ava was afraid Liz would burst in on the interview with the liaison officer and upset everything she might have achieved.

She went downstairs, saw them in the hall arguing quietly.

"Best to wait and see what she's been told, Mum," said Ryan.

"Wait? Wait? Don't you think we've waited long enough?" Ava had never heard her mother-in-law sound so angry.

"The liaison officer is with her, Liz," she said and was taken aback by the accusing glare she sent her way.

"It was your mother who did this!" she shouted. "Your mother who kept her, my little girl, all these years, just because she'd lost her own."

Ava bit her lip, not out of habit this time but to keep it from trembling. She'd never known anything but fondness, kindness from Liz and now she was what? Blaming her for her mother's crime? And more importantly, was Ryan also blaming her?

"I'm not sure that was her reason," said Ava.

"What else?" demanded Liz.

Why was Ryan not saying anything? Why was he not sticking up for her, telling his mother none of it was her doing? Could it be because he agreed with her?

"I think she was afraid to give her up for fear of what she might tell the police," Ava said. "Melanie was seven when she was abducted, old enough to describe the house, the people. They would investigate and find all the other bodies. But he was dead and Shirley couldn't kill her, not on her own."

"So you're saying she had compassion?" said Joe.

"No, I'm not saying that. I'm saying she didn't have the nerve to do it herself, otherwise she would have."

Liz took a step forward, closer to the staircase where Ava stood. She held herself stiffly, still with that look of accusation on her face.

"If you'd bothered to go and see her," she said, "you'd have found my Melanie. I would have had her back with me years ago."

Ava shook her head.

"I've been in that house for over a week now," she said, "and I saw no sign of her. She was living in a log cabin in the orchard."

Nobody spoke for a few moments. All three just stared up the stairs to where Ava still stood, four steps up, looking down at them.

"Where is she?" Ryan asked.

Ava nodded toward the living room and watched them go, noticed that her fists were clenching and her lip was trembling again. She bit down on it, hard. The woman she had thought of as a mother for four years now despised her, the man she loved had put a distance between them and his sister had no idea who she was. She'd lived most of her life in a log cabin at the bottom of the garden, among the trees where little or no sunlight could find its way in. She hadn't been to school, hadn't made friends, lived in fear of whoever was searching for her and had no idea she had a real family who loved her. And it was her fault! That bloody woman had caused all this.

Ava made up her mind then, on the spur of the moment. Shirley Fisher had ruined everything, just when Ava believed happiness was something she could have after all. She had destroyed her life, Ryan's life, Melanie's life and she could not be allowed to get away with it.

She watched Ryan and his parents go through to the living room, then she turned and made her way upstairs.

From the bathroom cabinet, she took the sleeping pills the doctor had prescribed for her when Gran died. Ava had had trouble sleeping back then; she worried how she would cope without Gran, but she hadn't taken many of the tablets and now she had most of the bottle left.

She took them to the kitchen and ground them into dust with the crusher. Pulling a bottle of fresh orange juice from the fridge, she poured it into a plastic bottle, added the powdered sleeping pills and replaced the lid. She shook the mixture as hard as she could then held the bottle up to the light to be sure the pills had all dissolved. There was enough there to fell an elephant. She smiled, remembered that old saying of Gran's, but it wasn't an elephant she wanted to fell. It was just an evil woman who did not deserve to live.

It never occurred to her, as she drove toward Lawston Manor, that by feeding this mixture to her mother she would be committing a crime, that she could end up behind bars for the rest of her life. She didn't think of that; she only thought of revenge. Her life was spoilt now, so what else was there to worry about?

Ryan no longer loved her; his parents had turned against her, probably thought she might turn out like Shirley, that evil must run in her family.

Ava drove through the wrought iron gates, passed the ornate gate posts, along the winding driveway and up to the front door, paying no attention to the people sitting at the tables on the lawn. She hardly noticed them; she had someone more important to seek out.

Before she left the car, she checked the bottle was still there, still upright, in her oversized handbag. She didn't want the juice to spill out and be wasted.

She didn't bother to lock the car. It was unlikely that any of the people here would steal it or its contents so she just slammed the door and strode up to the front door and the reception area.

"Mrs Kenyon," said the blonde receptionist.

Ava noticed that the girl seemed nervous today, not chirpy and over bubbly like she'd been before. She must have been watching the television news and knew about Mrs Kenyon's mother. She was probably lost for words.

"Is my mother inside?" Ava demanded.

Blondie took a deep breath.

"I'm afraid not, Mrs Kenyon," she replied. "The police took her away about an hour ago."

"The police? You mean they've arrested her?" Blondie nodded. "But she doesn't know what day of the week it is."

"I think they were told that," said the receptionist. "Let me call the doctor."

Ava waited impatiently, glancing occasionally at the sealed bottle in her handbag. Was this fate that had stopped her from carrying out her plan, or would she have another chance later on?

"Mrs Kenyon," said a deep African voice. "Come to my office, please. I will explain the situation."

He gestured Ava to a seat at his desk and sat himself down behind it, looking across at her with an impassive expression she could not analyse.

"Mrs Kenyon," he said. "Your mother's condition was very difficult to diagnose. I hope you understand that."

He seemed to waiting for an answer so Ava nodded her agreement.

"I expect it was," she said.

"We thought she was suffering from early onset Alzheimer's, but it seems likely now that she had a complete mental breakdown. Of course, had we known her home situation, we might have had a better idea of that."

"Her home situation?" said Ava angrily. "Is that what we're calling it? Are you quite sure she wasn't putting it on to escape blame for her 'home situation'?"

"I don't think that's likely," he replied. "It seems to me that it all got too much for her. I believe one of the children was still with her, hidden away from the world. The worry of what to do when she wanted to leave, perhaps realising what she had been a party to, caused a breakdown."

"So she was trying to commit suicide?" said Ava. "Trying to get hit by a fast moving vehicle. Seems about right; selfish to the end. Couldn't care less how many people were killed or maimed in the process."

"I don't believe that was her purpose," said the doctor. "Our psychiatric consultant has interviewed your mother at length and he believes that, in her muddled state, she was trying to stop a car. Perhaps she wanted a lift somewhere; who knows? Either way, the police seemed to think they might have more luck with their own specialist. She's at the main Cambridge police station, if you want to see her."

Ava allowed a little smile to touch her lips.

"I don't," she said. "I just hope she's coherent enough to stand trial."

***

When Ava arrived home she expected the house to be empty, expected that Melanie will have gone with Ryan and his parents back to her little pink bedroom. She'd forgotten about the roast chicken she'd prepared and hoped someone had thought to turn off the oven, or perhaps they had sat and eaten it. She'd made the dinner really for Melanie, so they might have taken it with them.

She was surprised to see them all sitting at the kitchen table. Ryan pushed back his chair and stood up, came to greet her.

"I've saved yours for you," he said.

Melanie sat quietly, looking bewildered. She gave Ava a hesitant smile, then she jumped up and ran to wrap her arms round her. Liz didn't smile; she only glared at Ava while Ryan went to the oven. Ava raised a hand.

"I'm not hungry," she said quietly.

"Where have you been?" he asked.

"Lawston Manor, to see her."

She didn't mention who she went to see as she wasn't sure what Melanie had been told. The girl still clung to her, like a lost child who suddenly sees someone she knows. It was an eerie feeling.

"And?" Ryan asked, pushing her plate back in the oven.

"The police are holding her for questioning."

She tried to ease herself away from the arms and body wrapped around her, but the girl just held on tighter.

"She wouldn't leave," Ryan said, nodding toward his sister. "Not till you came."

A little thrill of satisfaction tremored through Ava, but then she felt sure Melanie's attachment to her was just another reason for Liz to resent her. She gave Melanie a quick squeeze.

"Shall we go in the other room?" she asked. "Then you can tell me all about it."

Melanie nodded then moved away, started to make her way into the living room where they sat together on the sofa.

There was a huge box of chocolates on the side table and Ava could see Melanie's interest in it so she offered her one.

"Help yourself," she said. "I don't like chocolate, but someone bought it for us when we got married. A wedding present."

"Oh," said Melanie. "Was that recently?"

Ava nodded.

"It was. I wish we'd known where you were; we would have loved you to be there."

"Why? I have no idea who you are. That policewoman who came told me all sorts of things, but I'm not sure whether to believe her."

"Oh, Melanie. She told you no lie. That

woman you thought was your mother? She stole you away from your real mother and father when you were only seven. Do you remember nothing about that?"

Melanie fell silent, helped herself to another chocolate.

"I have thought sometimes that I remembered a woman talking to me, then taking me in her car. But when I told Moth … " She stopped and blushed. "I don't know what to call her now."

"Shirley," said Ava. "Her name's Shirley."

"Okay. Anyway, when I told her, she said it must have been a bad dream. I've had dreams where that's happened, but I took no notice. She said people were searching for me and they'd hurt me. I can't believe she lied."

"Didn't you think it was odd, that you never left that cabin?"

"It was all I knew. Moth … Shirley used to come in and see me every day, just for a few minutes, but she started really stocking up the freezer. I didn't think anything about it. If you hadn't found me when you did, I don't know what I would have done."

"I could have found you sooner, if I'd followed your music. I just thought it was one of the neighbours."

"That dinner was delicious, by the way," said Melanie. "I've never had anything like that before."

You have; you just don't remember it.

"I made it specially. I'm glad you enjoyed it."

"And that woman in the kitchen," said Melanie, "she really is my mother? That man is my father?"

"Yes, they are your parents and they've been miserable all these years, wondering what happened to you."

"And that gorgeous hunk?" she said with a grin. "He really is my brother?"

"Yes, he is and he would be off limits anyway. He's mine."

They laughed, but Ava saw the tears welling up in Melanie's eyes and she covered her hand with her own.

"This must be so confusing for you," she said. "And so sad. You are losing the only mother you remember."

"Will I be able to see her?"

"Do you want to? She took you away from your family and locked you up in a cabin down the end of the garden. Why do you want to see her?"

"I want to ask her why she did it."

Ava bit her lip, then stopped herself. She could almost hear Ryan telling her not to do that, but what could she say? How could she tell her that she was abducted by a paedophile, with the help of his wife, and that she's only alive because he didn't live long enough to hurt her. At least, that's what they all hoped.

And how could she tell her that Shirley probably kept her because she was alone and her own daughter had been taken away from her? How could she tell her that daughter was Ava, her brother's wife?

But perhaps that wasn't her reason.

Shirley was talking to the police; perhaps she was telling them the truth about what happened then, perhaps they would know after all.

"What is going to happen to me now?" said Melanie. "Can I stay with you?"

And have Liz and Joe think another member of my family has stolen her again.

Ava shook her head, her lips turned down as she fought against the need to bite them.

"They've waited a long time to have you home with them, Melanie," she answered. "It's not fair to them for you to stay here."

Melanie clutched Ava's hand until she winced from the pain of her nails digging into her flesh.

"I'm scared," she said. "I don't know them."

"You don't know me either."

"But you were the one who found me. Will you come with me at least?"

Ava nodded, not sure if she would be welcome but if that was what Melanie wanted, that was what was going to happen.

It was getting late and Melanie had no warm coat, so Ava took her up to her bedroom and let her choose a jacket from the wardrobe.

Downstairs, Liz was standing impatiently, her arms folded. She leapt forward when Melanie came down the stairs, ready to pull her into her arms, but Melanie halted her steps.

Why can't she see she is scaring the girl, that the way she is behaving is over the top?

"It's all right, Melanie," Ava said.

Liz was still giving her dirty looks and Ava knew in her heart that the closeness she'd always had with her mother-in-law was gone forever.

Melanie's hand went behind her and she clutched Ava's skirt.

"I don't know you," she said. "I want to stay here."

"No," said Liz. "You can't."

Yes, she can if she wants to. She's an adult now.

Ava saw that Liz's eyes were brimming with tears. This was not how she had imagined her reunion with her little girl would be, not at all.

"Melanie," Ava said, leaning over her shoulder where she still stood on the stairs. "Why don't we go to their house, see if it reminds you of anything. Your bedroom is there, just as you left it."

"Only if you come," Melanie said, causing Liz's mouth to turn down.

***

She wouldn't go in Ryan's car with Liz and Joe; she insisted on going with Ava, sat in the front passenger seat and silently watched the scenery go by.

"You okay?" said Ava.

Melanie nodded.

"I suppose. If that woman really is my mother, what's she going to do? Is she going to shut me away in the garden, give me a television and a DVD player, some books perhaps?"

Ava checked her mirror, saw nothing following her and pulled over to the kerb. She switched off the ignition and turned to her forlorn passenger.

"Is that what happened?" she asked.

Melanie nodded, swallowed back more tears but they escaped anyway.

"I lied before, when I said she came to see me every day. She didn't. I suppose it was about once a week and she never stayed, just came in long enough to fill up the fridge and the freezer, sometimes bring me stuff, like the DVD player. And the clothes, of course, but never anything new."

"You poor thing. You must have been so lonely."

"I asked her for a pet, a dog or a cat, but she said she didn't want the bother of burying something else when it died." She turned to give Ava a dejected look. "I never did know what she meant by that."

I do. I know what she meant by it. Obviously that policewoman didn't tell her the worst of it.

"Liz won't treat you like that, I promise. She loves you. It broke her heart to lose you."

"Then why didn't she come looking for me?" Melanie demanded.

"She did. She just didn't know where to look." Something occurred to Ava then, something she hadn't really noticed before. "Tell me, Melanie," she said. "You didn't seem very surprised when I told you she wasn't your mother."

"She said she was," said Melanie. "But she didn't behave like the mothers in the films she used to bring for me. Or the books I read."

"She taught you to read?"

Melanie gave a short ironic laugh.

"I could already read. I just taught myself from there, really, and as the books got harder, I trained myself to keep up with them. I didn't have much else to do, did I?"

"But she was never cruel to you? Never unkind?"

"Unless you call locking me up in a garden shed and never letting me out cruel. Unless you call telling me it wasn't safe outside unkind."

Ava reached out and pulled her into her arms, kissed her cheek and tasted the salt from her wet cheeks.

"We best get going," she said. "They'll wonder where we are."

"I don't want to go. How do I know she won't be the same?"

"Sweetheart, you're an adult now. It's up to you what you do, but please, give them a chance. They yearned for this day for so long."

Melanie nodded, sank back into her seat while Ava started the engine and continued the journey to her in-laws' house. She knew that if Melanie insisted on coming home with Ava, Liz would be even more resentful toward her. But what the hell could she do to stop her? She couldn't refuse; that would be cruel.

The front door was standing open when they arrived, everyone else already inside and turning on the lights. It was getting late, twilight making the tatty clothing worn by Melanie to be eerie somehow. First thing tomorrow Ava would take her out shopping.

She led Melanie into the living room, where everyone waited, seated on the sofa and the armchairs and looking up expectantly when they entered. But Melanie wasn't interested in making herself comfortable; the first thing she saw was the portrait of the wedding group, with herself in a lacy pink bridesmaid gown, her blonde curls shining in the sunlight and looking just as she did now, this minute, nineteen years old and a beautiful young woman.

She approached it with wonderment in her soft blue eyes and reached up to run her fingers over the surface.

"That's me," she said. "That's me, but I wasn't there. How could that be?" She spun around and stared at Liz accusingly. "Did you take photographs of me? Did you sneak into the garden and take pictures through the window, just to do this?"

"No," all four said at once.

"So you must have known where I was, mustn't you? You could have rescued me then. So you didn't want me there!" She pointed at the wedding portrait. "You just wanted an image of me to show your friends."

"Melanie, that's not what happened," said Ava.

"I can see what's going to happen here. You just wanted to keep it up long enough to get sympathy from everyone. 'What a shame Melanie can't be here'; I've seen that sort of thing in my films."

"Melanie," Ava said firmly. "That picture was aged, using computer software. It's clever that it turned out to be so accurate, but please believe me; there is nothing we'd all have liked more than to have you there. I promise."

"Computer software?" she repeated in a hoarse whisper. "What does that mean?"

There was so much this girl needed to learn to keep up with her contemporaries, so much Ava was longing to teach her, if only she had the chance.

"I'll show you all that," said Ryan. "Just give me time."

Melanie shook her head.

"I want Ava to show me," she said.

Again, Liz scowled and she glanced at Joe. She hadn't been able to gauge his reaction at all, had no idea about his feelings in all this.

Liz was on her feet now, moving rapidly toward her daughter, her arms out. Ava held her breath, wondering what Melanie would do. It would be too hurtful if she were to move away again. But she allowed the embrace, although she didn't return it.

Now Liz was crying, hugging Melanie to her, soaking her hair with her tears.

"Do you want a drink?" Joe said, standing up.

"No, thank you," Melanie replied. "I just want to go home with Ava."

With Ava. Not Ava and Ryan, not her brother, just Ava. Liz will never forgive me.

"But don't you want to see your room?" said

Liz. "It's just as you left it."

"A room for a seven year old?" said Melanie.

Melanie's thin body had gone rigid and that was when Ava realised what she was afraid of. She wasn't going to enter any place that could be locked from the outside.

"You ought to look," said Ava. "It might remind you of things, make this whole thing easier for you."

Melanie moved out of Liz's embrace and took Ava's hand, held on to it tightly.

"Only if you come," she said.

"No!" It was too much for Liz. She had waited years for this and now her own child wanted someone else instead of her and that someone else was the daughter of the woman who had kept her all this time.

"Mum, please," said Ryan. He got to his feet and put his arm around her but she shrugged him off. She'd never done that before, never in his entire life. "Let her have Ava with her if it helps her."

"Hasn't that family stolen enough of her life from us?" Liz shouted. "First her nonce father stole her away, then her stupid mother decides to hang on to her and I can't imagine why. She quite obviously wasn't much of a mother to her own kid."

"No, she wasn't," said Ava tearfully. "That's

why I loved you so much."

CHAPTER SIXTEEN

Ryan stayed at his parents' house that night. Melanie seemed happier with him there, but she insisted on sleeping on the sofa. She wasn't going to go into that bedroom. Ava went home; it was glaringly obvious to her that she would not be welcome with them and that hurt more than anything.

The following morning she set out early to go to the police station. She wanted to see this woman who gave birth to her, wanted to see if she would explain to her how she could have turned her own child over to a pervert, how she could have married him and most of all, what had happened to the three baby boys in those tiny graves in the garden.

And Melanie? Why did she keep her? She could have put her on a bus, taken her to a hospital and left her there. A child of seven would have been unlikely to lead the police to Primrose Cottage after a bus journey. But Shirley Fisher had no idea what a child of seven might remember; she knew nothing about children, except what they could be used for.

The inspector heard her voice and came out of the back office to greet her. His expression was grim and he looked as though he had been up all night. Perhaps he had.

"How's the girl?" he asked as soon as he appeared.

"Melanie? Confused, bewildered, terrified."

"What was the story?" asked the inspector. "I haven't been able to get any sense out of Shirley. Whenever I ask about her, she just shrugs."

"It seems she locked her in that log cabin, gave her a video player, then later a DVD player and a telly that wouldn't get any signal for actual programmes. I suppose she didn't want her watching the news. She kept her fed, clothed in her own old clothes, but there was no contact. Poor kid was completely isolated."

"Well, Shirley's not talking. Just keeps saying it was nothing to do with her."

"Isn't that what Rose West said?" said Ava with a note of cynicism. "How many bodies have you found?"

The inspector's mouth turned down in a grim line; the look of disgust was almost palpable.

"At least fifty so far," he said. "All girls, all under ten and all in the attic. The only ones buried were the three baby boys."

Ava bit her lip, stopped herself, then wondered why it mattered any more.

"And it's my fault," she said.

"Why is it your fault? You didn't even live there."

"No, but it's what she said and she's right. If I hadn't told my gran what was happening, she wouldn't have taken me away and he'd have had no need for all the others." She paused for breath and the inspector touched her arm for a split second, then withdrew it. "That's what she said. That's what she told me."

He briefly closed his eyes, sighed deeply.

"I'm not surprised you didn't want anything to do with her," he said. "But, whatever she said, none of it was your fault."

"Can I see her?"

"Why would you want to?"

"I need to know if she meant it."

"Well, I can't get anything out of her. Maybe you'll have more luck. She's going to prison, no matter what she says."

Ava nodded. *Thank heavens for small mercies.*

"Is she coherent, then?"

"I don't know, to be honest. She's making no sense, but I'm not convinced."

She made her way into the interview room where her mother sat at a well used wooden table and a police officer in uniform stood in the corner, almost to attention. Ava slid into the chair opposite, wondering where to begin.

"Why?" she asked at last. "Why did you help him?"

"I loved him," Shirley replied. "I loved him

for most of my life. I'd have done anything for him."

"It seems you did," Ava replied. "How could you? All those children?"

"Was what he wanted. I grew up, that was the trouble, then we had plans. We were going to have girls, lots of them."

At this, Ava bit her lips again, fought back the tears that gathered in her throat.

"And I was the first?"

"Yeah and a great disappointment you were," she spat. "We tried for years after that, but nothing happened. He was too old, that was the trouble."

Ava was unaware that a man's age could affect anything when it came to conception but she could be wrong.

"T'weren't my fault," Shirley snapped angrily. "I did my best, didn't I? He reckoned those boys were my fault, too."

"The boys," said Ava. "The baby boys in those graves, three of them. What happened to them?"

Shirley grinned, the sort of evil grin one might see in a horror film from the villain of the piece.

"What d'you think happened to them?" She answered. "Weren't no use to him, were they? He wasn't into boys."

"And you did nothing to stop him? Nothing

to protect your own babies?"

She was quiet for a few seconds and Ava thought she saw a little spark of conscience showing through.

"I couldn't," she said. "He was the only one there. He took them."

"And me? You knew what he was planning, but you did nothing to stop him."

"I told you; I loved him."

"I doubt you even know what the word means," said Ava.

Shirley shrugged, clasped her hands together on the table. Ava wondered why she wasn't wearing handcuffs and ankle chains, but that was in America, wasn't it? We're much more trusting here, much too soft in England.

"You were the one who spoilt things," said Shirley bitterly. "Going blabbing to my mother about it all. He told you to keep quiet! So did I."

Ava swallowed back that painful bunch of tears.

"What about Melanie?"

"She was the one that did for him," said Shirley. "Wouldn't stop screaming 'Ryan!' whoever he is. She bit him, you know. Actually bit him on his hand."

"Good for her."

Shirley glared at her.

"It was the shock, gave him a heart attack. I

had to put her in the shed down the garden, that one where you used to play. I couldn't have the ambulance people finding her, could I?"

"And after they'd gone?"

"I was up the hospital for two days. Then I couldn't make up my mind what to do with her. I wanted to kill her, like she'd done to him, but I didn't think I could. Not out of any soppiness; just because I'm not strong enough."

"So you had the cabin built?"

"Not straight away. I was too upset, grieving for my Tom and I hated that kid so much. But then I got to thinking how much damage she could cause me if I let her go. So I looked after her."

That's what you call looking after her?

"And why were you wandering around the motorway?"

"I wasn't wandering," she said. "I was trying to get a lift."

"Where to?"

"Anywhere. I'd just had enough and I wanted to bugger off, go somewhere where nobody knows me."

"What about Melanie? What had you planned to do with her?"

"Hadn't made up my mind. I stocked up for her and I thought, if no one found her, it'd solve my problem. And if they did find her, well, by then she thought she belonged there."

She laughed then, but it wasn't a pleasant laugh; it was a laugh that sent a shiver down Ava's spine, made her want to jump up and run out of the room.

"How did you get involved with him? How did Gran and Grandad let it happen?"

For the first time, she started to lay some blame at Gran's door. If she'd been paying proper attention, it could never have happened, could it? But they just let that man alone with their little girl until he had her wrapped so far round his little finger, she didn't know she had mind, much less how to use it.

But that was excusing her. At some point, she must have realised the evil she was doing. She could have stopped then.

Ava thought of all the women who suffered years of abuse from their husbands and were too afraid to leave, too cowed to protect themselves or their children. But that wasn't the case here, was it? Shirley didn't help him out of fear; she did it out of love, an obsessive, unhealthy love that started when she was too young to know right from wrong.

Ava pushed the chair back and got to her feet, still not sure whether to blame her or pity her. Whichever it was, she hated her. And now she had lost Liz, the only mother she ever loved, and it was all the fault of this evil woman.

"You going?" said Shirley. "Just when we were getting cosy."

In the corridor, she almost ran into the inspector who had been watching the interview on a computer screen in the next room.

"Sorry," he said.

"I didn't expect anything else. She certainly doesn't seem like anyone with mental health problems."

"I think she put that on. We've interviewed the driver who nearly ran her down, the one who phoned us in the first place. He said she didn't seem too bad till she realised it was the police he was ringing, then by the time our boys got there she was behaving like she was senile. She even managed to fool the doctors at Lawston Manor."

"Just lock her up and throw away the key," said Ava. "She's ruined everything. I hope she rots."

***

"I want Ava!"

Melanie sat with her arms folded, a childish scowl on her face. Liz and Joe exchanged glances.

"Stop behaving like a child," said Joe.

"But she is a child, love," said his wife. "She's had no education, no experience of the world, and no love."

"I am here, you know," said Melanie. "I can hear you. And I'm not a child; Ava told me so."

"Ava will see you later," Ryan said soothingly. "She had to go home last night."

"Why? Why couldn't I go with her?" A crafty look appeared on Melanie's face as she leaned toward her brother. "She told me I was an adult and could do what I wanted," she said. "I don't want to stay here. I want to go with Ava."

Ryan glanced at his mother and saw the tears gathering in her eyes, saw her mouth turn down in a grim line.

"That's it then," she shouted. "She's told her that so she can take her away, like her pervert mother!"

Melanie looked at her suspiciously, her eyes narrowed.

"What do you mean?" she asked quietly. "What do you mean *just like her mother*?"

"Oh, she didn't tell you that much then," said Liz, then felt guilty that she had raised her voice to her, when she was really so pleased to have her back. "I'm sorry," she said.

She slid into the chair beside Melanie, reached across the table and touched the arm that was still folded across her chest. Letting her hand rest there for a moment, she hoped for some response, hoped that her little girl would unfold her arms and perhaps reach out for her real mother. Making a concession, Melanie unfolded her arms and stretched them out in front of her across the table. It was better than nothing, Liz thought.

"Well?" said Melanie. "What did you mean?"

"The woman …" Liz began, but knew she would not be able to keep the bitterness out of her voice. Her eyes met Ryan's in appeal and he sat at the table, on the other side of his sister, and took her hand.

"The woman who has kept you prisoner all these years, the woman you thought was your mother, well, she is Ava's mother."

Melanie shook her head, a gesture of denial.

"How can that be? Has she been living in that big house all this time? Have you?"

"No, no." He wasn't sure where to begin. "It's more complicated than that," he finally said. "Ava went to live with her grandmother when she was only six. She knew nothing about her mother or her father until Social Services contacted her about her. It was when she was going through the stuff in the house and garden that she found you."

Melanie looked at Liz, saw the tears that had begun to brim over onto her cheeks, and finally took her hand. She could not know how that simple gesture brought an ache to Liz's heart that threatened to stop it.

"I'm sorry," Melanie said. "I haven't thought about how all this must be for you."

"It doesn't matter," Liz said. She desperately wanted to hug her, hold her in her arms and never let go, but she knew that it would probably only push her away. "We all thought you were dead. We only hoped to …" No, she wouldn't talk corpses and funerals. "We couldn't believe it when Ryan told us you were alive."

"And who was it told me, Mum?" Ryan said. "Who was it found Melanie, brought her back to us. You're not being fair to Ava."

"I don't think this is the time or the place to argue about it," said Joe. "We have our girl home. That's all that matters now."

"And if Ava had bothered to even check on her mother, even when her father died, we'd have had her home a lot sooner. Christ Almighty! We'd have had her home straight away!"

***

It was over. The gleam of happiness Ava had seen in her future was gone, snuffed out by the appearance of a woman she had thought never to see again. Hell, she hadn't even given her a thought in twenty years, had totally forgotten that she existed at all, and because she'd decided to play demented, pretend to be senile, Ava had lost everything.

They had Melanie back, so they should all be happy now, including Ryan. They didn't need Ava any more and neither did he. And Liz was right; if Ava had bothered to remember she'd got a mother, she might have found Melanie. When Gran told her that her father was dead, she felt nothing. Why should she feel anything when she had no memory of him, none at all. She must have blotted him out; her mind must have rescued her from the horror. She had heard that happened sometimes.

If she had remembered him, she would also have remembered what he did to her and she wouldn't have cared that he was dead. She'd have been glad. She might even have remembered Shirley's part in it.

As it was, Ava felt nothing. As far as she was concerned, Gran was the only mother she'd had or wanted. Something buried deep in her memory must have been warning her to stay away and she had no choice other than to heed that warning.

But Liz was right, wasn't she? They were all

right. It was her abandonment of her mother that had kept Melanie away from them for so long, her neglect that had caused that little girl to grow to adulthood locked away among the trees with no human contact save that of a bitter, twisted woman who blamed her for the death of her husband and who only kept her alive because she had no choice.

They would always blame Ava, wouldn't they? Ryan's family would always blame her. She thought it ironic that, when she found photographs of Melanie in those suitcases, Ava believed it would damage her marriage and her relationship with her in-laws if Melanie turned out to have been taken by her father. That was why she burned the photographs, in the hope that they would never know she'd found them. She was happy when she found her alive. She thought they'd be so pleased and she was happy for them.

It was a miracle and she had no clue then how something so wonderful could have the power to end her world.

In the spare room she found a suitcase. It was a modern, canvas suitcase, dark blue with a floral pattern and a zip fastener. It also had a handle and wheels so it held no resemblance to the cases in Primrose Cottage, the ones that had served as tombs for countless innocent children.

But still she shuddered as she put it on the bed, still she hesitated before she opened it, still she felt a sense of deep dread and fear of what she might find inside.

It was empty, completely empty but for a couple of receipts from their honeymoon. Was that really only a couple of weeks ago? That wonderful Florida holiday where she grew even closer to Ryan. But he was gone now. He didn't take her part when his mother turned on her. He, too must blame Ava.

First Shirley blamed her for telling Gran the secret so that he needed more. Was that fair? She was helpless and she cried out for help. He would have needed more anyway, wouldn't he? She could reason her way out of that accusation, but not the people she loved turning on her.

And they were right, weren't they? Had she gone to her father's funeral she might have discovered Melanie. She was still in the playhouse then; that wasn't hidden by the trees. Shirley wouldn't have invited anyone back to the house, that was for certain, but if Ava had been determined, she could have forced her way in.

But she didn't; she stayed away because she didn't care about either of them. Gran didn't go to the funeral, Gran didn't look in on her own daughter. If she had, she might have found

Melanie.

All these thoughts ran through her mind as she packed her clothes into the suitcase. She only intended to take what she'd need for a few days and stuff that wouldn't crease up in the case. She'd come back for the rest when she'd found somewhere permanent to live.

She had paid for this house with the money that Gran had left her, but that wasn't important now. Ryan could have it all; she wouldn't argue about it.

Her eyes wandered around the bedroom and she swallowed the tears that had gathered in her throat. It was all going to be so perfect. She had her perfect husband, his parents who loved her, and she was prepared to mourn the loss of Melanie with them. She had seen a bright future, with children of her own, and she would have known then exactly how they felt about losing their own.

She remembered her thoughts then, how she had believed that everything would be more than perfect if Melanie could be found alive. That must have been some kind of cosmic joke! The universe having a good laugh at her expense!

In the bathroom, she gathered her toothbrush and paste, her face wash and other toiletries, held them in her hands as she walked back into the bedroom. But Ryan was there, staring into the suitcase as though he'd never seen anything like it before.

"What's this?" he said.

She stood for a moment, just looking at him, wanting to fall into his arms but knowing she would not be welcome. Then she walked forward, dumped the toiletries into the case on top of her clothes and turned to face him.

"I'm leaving, Ryan," she said. "You have Melanie back and I know you must blame me, like your mother does. And she's right. When the old man died I thought only of myself. I could have gone to her then, couldn't I? And I'd have found your sister twelve years ago."

He was shaking his head but he made no move to reach for her. So she was right then; he did blame her.

"No, Ava. You can't leave me. I've just got my sister back and now I must wonder what's happened to my wife?"

"You won't need to wonder. I'll let you know where I am, but everything we had has gone, don't you see that? Melanie would never have suffered as she did if I hadn't been thinking about myself. You know that, your parents know it and Melanie will know it soon. She thinks she can trust me, but she'll blame me too when she finds out the truth. We can't come back from this, Ryan."

She turned back to her suitcase and began to find places for her toiletries in the pockets. Zipping it up, she felt the silence, like the chill from a snowstorm, the need to hear him speak running through her veins.

She was pulling the heavy case toward her when she felt his hand on hers, bringing a small amount of warmth to that chill. Turning, she looked up into his eyes.

"I'm right, aren't I?" she said. "There's no coming back from this."

"No," he said. "No, you're not right. I can't say I haven't felt a flicker of resentment; that would be a lie. But, darling, we have something special. We can overcome this, we can. Please, stay. Please let's try."

Ava released the suitcase handle and turned to face him. She knew he didn't really believe his own words, and she doubted them, too. But she was going to stay; there was nothing else she could do. Whatever happened, she wasn't sure she could live without Ryan.

CHAPTER SEVENTEEN

Ava refused to go with Ryan to visit his parents. She knew they blamed her and she knew they would likely never get over that. She was beginning to blame herself because what they said was true; had she bothered etc etc. And she couldn't bear the idea of that sweet, naïve girl blaming her too. And she would, wouldn't she?

Ryan blamed her. He would never say it, but she knew. They made love last night but it was different, more distant somehow. She'd had a family, the family she'd always wanted and it had been snatched away from her by the evil old bitch who gave birth to her. Or Gran. She could have said something; she must have suspected, knowing that all those local children were being taken. She could have reported her suspicions to the police. Perhaps she was more concerned about the scandal than the welfare of those girls, with the pain of their families.

Ava had no real idea if her Gran ever visited Shirley after she took Ava away from her, but she was her daughter. It would have been natural to at least phone her, wouldn't it? She couldn't help wondering if Gran really had no suspicion of this man who was so interested in her little girl. Certainly an unrelated grown man paying too much attention to a little girl would cause eyebrows to raise nowadays, but back then? And he was her grandfather's best friend.

Then she recalled the more recent, famous case, a well known television personality who had molested his neighbour's daughter, his own daughter's best friend, for years. Nobody had suspected, nobody had thought anything strange about him.

Would Gran had kept in touch with Shirley? Or did she consider Ava to be her second chance to bring up a little girl in safety?

She still had those crushed up sleeping pills, dissolved in that little bottle of orange juice. But Shirley Fisher was behind bars and out of reach. She would be tried, she would be given a life sentence if there was any justice and she wouldn't be a popular addition to the prison population.

She heard Ryan's car, she heard voices and her heart leapt, wondering who he had brought with him. She couldn't face another confrontation with his mother. Making her way to the front window, her heart leapt again when she saw his passenger getting out of the car. It was Melanie.

Dressed in a brand new pair of jeans and an expensive looking blouse, she had a leather jacket draped over her shoulders. Her hair had been professionally cut to enhance her gorgeous blonde curls. She wore no make up; her skin was fresh and clear, though still pale and she looked stunning.

"You've been shopping," Ava said.

"Yes. My real mother took me this morning. She said she'll get lots more, that we can go to the shops in town or even in London."

"You look beautiful, really gorgeous."

"Thank you," Melanie said. "Ryan said you would be able to teach me how to use make up."

Ryan said; not Liz, not his mother.

"Of course I can," Ava said. "We'll use mine for now, then we can get you some of your own."

"I'd rather buy my own straight away," said Melanie. "Can you take me? Or do you have something else to do?"

"Nothing. I've told my manager I need more time off. We can spend all day if you like. I'd love to take you."

"Do you want me to come?" asked Ryan.

Is he afraid to leave his sister alone with me?

"No," answered Melanie before Ava had a chance to say anything. "Nobody needs a man with them when they shop for make up."

It sounded like a joke, but her tone was not one of humour. Ava felt an underlying ambiance of anger behind the words.

They both waved to Ryan as they pulled away from the kerb and straight away, Melanie spoke.

"Why didn't you go to your father's funeral?" she demanded. "Why didn't you go to see if your mother was all right? You would have found me, wouldn't you? When I was still a frightened child, you would have found me."

Ava checked her mirror, indicated and moved over to the kerb. She wasn't prepared to have this conversation while she was driving. She switched off the engine and turned to face her.

"Do you think for one minute if I'd known you were there, if I'd known anything was there, I wouldn't have gone?"

"But you just abandoned her."

"As she abandoned me, left me to be molested by a perverted father who cared for nothing but his own satisfaction." She was angry now. Even though she'd half expected this, she didn't think the accusation was justified. "She only had me for him to play with. She told me so."

Melanie was slowly shaking her head.

"She was always all right to me."

At least she didn't tell you how much she hated you. Briefly, Ava wondered why.

"Perhaps she was, but you'd have seen a different side to her if he'd been there. I know you suffered, Love; I know you spent twelve years of your life locked away with no company save the television. But you were luckier than all those other little girls he abducted."

Melanie frowned, a puzzled frown that told Ava she knew nothing about those others. Nobody had told her and she wouldn't know about Ava's brothers either, would she? She wouldn't know about the tiny graves on the other side of the orchard.

"What others?" she said quietly.

"You were not the only one," Ava said. "You were only the last of many and if he hadn't dropped dead, you wouldn't be here now. You'd be one more corpse in a suitcase."

Melanie's eyes were swimming and Ava pulled her into her arms and hugged her.

"I'm sorry," she said. "Perhaps I shouldn't have told you that, but you need to know how lucky you are."

***

She dropped Melanie off at her home, but didn't go in. Liz was staring out of the window when they arrived and Ava had the strong feeling she had been there the whole time they'd been gone. She waved, but got no response save a scowl.

"Are you coming in?" Melanie asked.

"No. I won't be welcome."

"She's got to get over it, hasn't she? You're my brother's wife." She paused and gave Ava a huge smile. "That sounds really weird to me. All my life, or at least the part I can remember, I thought I had no one except …"

"Perhaps she'll understand one day," said Ava, gently touching her arm. "I'm glad you do though. That's the important thing."

"No, it's not. I was rescued and brought home, you found me and by so doing you lost the respect of my real parents. That's not right and it makes me feel ashamed. It makes me think everyone would have been better off if I hadn't been found."

Ava wasn't going to tell her that she'd probably lost Ryan's respect as well, or at least a large part of it.

"Oh, Melanie, you must never think like that. You don't know how the family have suffered all these years, not knowing whether you were dead or alive."

"But I haven't suffered, not really."

But she'd have escaped and left you there to die.

Ava thought it, but wasn't going to say it.

"Your childhood was stolen from you," she said. "Your education, your freedom, all gone forever. Because I didn't bother to check on my mother."

Melanie was silent for a few minutes, glanced toward the house to see Liz still looking anxiously for her child to come home. Ava supposed she would feel the same if she were in her place.

"She'll come round," said Melanie. "Right now she'll do anything for me." She opened the car door. "Thank you for taking me shopping. Now I can have a go at the make up and see what sort of mess I make of it."

She gave Ava that huge smile again and Ava watched as she went towards the front door, watched as Liz disappeared from the window and opened that door, watched as she threw her arms round Melanie and hugged her tight. Ava would never have that contact again.

***

When they were out buying make up and perfume, Ava had treated herself to a new handbag. It caught her eye in the window of the leather goods shop next door and she felt an impulse to own it.

When she had dropped Melanie off and got home, she poured some apple juice and sat down to inspect her new purchase. She pulled out the paper that was keeping it in shape and began to empty her old bag, ready to begin using the new one.

That was when she found the little bottle of orange juice that she had hoped to feed to her mother. She'd taken the little bottle with her to the nursing home, but was too late because the police had already taken her away.

She ought to throw the bottle in the rubbish, but she didn't want to. She might still get an opportunity, it was always possible.

Ava turned to the front window when she heard a car pulling into the driveway. It was the police inspector; she thought she had seen the last of him, at least until the trial.

She dropped the bottle into her new handbag. She'd tip it down the sink when he'd gone. She wouldn't need it now, because Shirley Fisher was going away for a very long time, probably for the rest of her life. Prisoners didn't like child molesters and murderers and they liked female ones even less. Ava could be satisfied that her mother would get her just desserts for her crimes and she would have a bad time in there.

A few days ago, when she was alone, she found on You Tube a documentary about the Moors murderer, Myra Hindley, and the bad time she had in Holloway Prison. It was a long time ago, but attitudes hadn't changed. Ava could be satisfied that her mother would suffer similarly.

She opened the front door before the Inspector had reached it and held it open for him to enter. His expression was sombre, gloomy even, enough to stab at her heart as she could see something was wrong.

"What's up?" she asked quickly.

"Can we sit down?"

When a police officer asked to sit down, it meant bad news. She'd watched enough detective programmes to know that. She led him into the living room and gestured to the sofa while she took an armchair close by.

"Well?" she demanded.

"You're not going to like this," he said. "Your mother's condition has worsened. The psychiatrist says she's not fit to stand trial."

Ava leaned forward, her hands clasped together, a grim line of fury forming on her lips.

"No!" she yelled. "She's putting it on, can't they see that? She was putting it on before; she was coherent enough when she spoke to me. Did you tell them? Do they know how she planned to leave, to run away and leave Melanie to starve to death?"

"I told them that, of course I did. But they think they know best and I can't do anything about it. I'm sorry."

"So she's going to get away with it to satisfy some idiot's professional vanity."

"Two psychiatrists have examined her and both agree."

"Where is she? What'll happen to her?"

"She's been returned to Lawston Manor for now, until a more suitable, secure place can be found. Something like Broadmoor might do, but she isn't insane; she's senile and that's different."

"No, she's not senile. She's a crafty old cow who knows precisely what she's doing. She shouldn't be in that nice cosy place, she shouldn't have those comforts."

"If it's any consolation, she won't be staying there. She'll probably end up in a cheaper place, at least for now. While her house is still a crime scene, it can't be sold and it's going to take us months to go through it all."

He got to his feet.

"As I said, I can do nothing about it." He made his way to the door. "I wish I could."

She showed him out, bit her lip, swallowed her anger and picked up her car keys, then gathered up her new handbag containing the little bottle of orange juice.

Time to pay Mother a visit.

Thank you for Reading …. I hope you have enjoyed this story and if you have, please consider my other books.

Ye Olde Antique Shoppe *– A time slip series*

The Edward V Coin
The Anne Boleyn Necklace
The Ripper Rings
The Roman Bracelet
The Confederate Cap
The Tarot Cards and the Rosary
The Miniature and the Swastika
The Egyptian Headdress
Letter from the Tudor Court
Hitler's Notebook

Historical fiction/romance:

The Romany Princess
The Wronged Wife
To Catch a Demon
The Gorston Widow
The Crusader's Widow
The Minstrel's Lady (winner of the 2017 e-festival of words Best Romance)
The Adulteress
Conquest
A Man in Mourning
The Cavalier's Pact
Shed No Tears
The Outcasts
The Secret of Ainsley Gate
Daughters of Trengowan
The Million Dollar Bride

Factual:
The Loves of the Lionheart
For the Love of Anne

Series:

Holy Poison – a six book series telling of the ordinary people who lived through the brutal reign of Bloody Mary

The Judas Pledge
The Flawed Mistress
The Viscount's Birthright
Betrayal
The Heretics
Consequences

Summerville – Sequel to Holy Poison

Pestilence – A three book series set around the Black Death

The Second Wife
The Scent of Roses
Once Loved (winner of the 2018 e-festival of words Best Historical Novel)

The Elizabethans – A three book series following the lives of three noble brothers and what they sacrificed for love

The Earl's Jealousy
The Viscount's Divorce
Lord John's Folly

Knight's Acre

Book One – Till Death Do Us Part

Book Two – The Forgotten Witness
Book Three – The Countess of Harrisford

The Hartleighs of Somersham – a Regency tale

A Match of Honour (winner of the e-festival of words 2018 best Historical Romance)
Lady Penelope's Frenchman

Other Books:

Old Fashioned Values
The Surrogate Bride (a historical fantasy)

Mirielle
The Longest Shadow

The Tale of the Missing Bridegroom – A Charlotte Chase Mystery

Short Stories:

Taking Care of Mother
The Gatecrasher

If you would like to receive notification of future publications, as well as special offers, please sign up to my newsletter here Or visit my website at www.margaretbrazearbooks.com

Printed in Great Britain
by Amazon